I0687548

When Swallows Fall

by

Gloria Davidson Marlow

When Swallows Fall

Cover Art by *Tina Lynn Stout*

The Wild Rose Press, Inc.
PO Box 708
Adams Basin, NY 14410-0708
Visit us at www.thewildrosepress.com

Publishing History
First American Rose Edition, 2013
Print ISBN 978-1-62830-112-0
Digital ISBN 978-1-62830-113-7

Published in the United States of America

"How did Desi die, Cade?"

He lifted his head, his face mere inches from mine. Emotion clouded his gaze, and he opened his mouth as if he meant to answer me. Instead, a low moan escaped him and he caught my mouth in the hungry kiss I had dreamed of for six years' worth of lonely nights. For just a moment, the reason for that loneliness was completely forgotten.

A cry rent the air, and I jerked away from Cade, guilt and alarm whipping through me in equal measures as I turned to stare at the maid who had finally returned with the broom and dustpan.

"Oh, Mr. Scott, forgive me, please."

"No need for apologies, Susan," Cade said, bringing the woman's stammering apology to an end. He looked at me, his eyes shadowed with pain. "I'm the one who should be sorry. I'll see you at supper, Ophelia."

I was left standing in the hall with the maid, who stared at me with open disdain. Her voice was sharp and cold when she spoke.

"I thought you were Mrs. Scott, you know. Kissing her husband like that. It made me think Kathleen was right and she had come back from the grave after all."

"People don't come back from the grave, Susan," I retorted, hoping my haughtiness hid my shame. If Desi were to come back to haunt the halls of the home where she'd died, I was fairly certain what I'd just done would be reason enough for me to be her target.

Praise for Gloria Davidson Marlow

"*SWEET SACRIFICES* grabs you right from the beginning and doesn't let go. A surprisingly good mystery with some suspense and clean romance adding interest to the story.... The setting is a well done historical.... I loved how the story developed, and the little twists and turns played within the characters' relationships...emotional, not just romantic...*SWEET SACRIFICES* is wonderful to read."

~*Vicky, Sizzling Hot Book Reviews (5 Hearts)*

"*SWEET SACRIFICES* ensnares the reader's emotions and imagination with heartbreaking scenes of Kendal's past when she is at the mercy of circumstances she cannot control. [With] compelling, interwoven subplots that reveal Kendall's strength, courage, and capacity to love...the story, so full of sacrifices, becomes a story of amazing, euphoric love that is strong, patient, and true. This story shows the flaws and foibles of human nature, but it, most of all, shows love that overcomes all."

~*Camellia, Long and Short Romance Reviews(4 Books)*

"Turning a tangled web of deceit and pain into a sweet love story is not an easy thing to do.... Immediately drawn to her characters and driven by the constant mystery surrounding them, I couldn't put the book down.... Seamlessly blended into the romance is a mystery. Ms Marlow has written a well-developed story with multi-dimensional characters, each with enough depth to stand on their own. The characters seem real, the issues authentic, and the conclusion an unexpected happily ever after. This is a sweet romance and a great read."

~*Rebecca, The Romance Reviews (4 Stars)*

Dedication

To Jason, Forrest, Melissa, and Curtis

Chapter One

Ophelia and Desdemona. Those were the names my mother whispered as the midwife placed my newborn self in the crook of one of her arms and my twin sister in the other. According to the story my father was told by the midwife, and which he relayed to us many times over the ensuing years, they were the last words my mother spoke before passing quietly into the life beyond this mortal plane.

I would wonder as we grew to adulthood if my mother, in those last moments of her life, caught a glimpse into the future, or if it was simply her love of all things Shakespearean that fueled her desire to name us for two such tragic females. As she stared down at her tiny infant daughters, had she seen two women destined for heartache from the moment they were born? Or, as my father explained, was she simply a country vicar's wife, enamored with the works of Shakespeare and dazzled by a recent trip to the theater?

Whatever her reasons, my father honored what was apparently her last wish and wrote those names on our birth records. He rarely used the names, however, preferring to call us Desi and Fee, and raising us in a quiet little hamlet near the James River, ninety miles south of the bright lights of Richmond and the theatrical tragedies that had so enthralled our mother.

On the clear autumn day that John Bailey, the local

1

constable and my late father's closest friend, found me planting flower bulbs in my spring garden, I would wonder again if my mother had foreseen the tragedy that was about to unfold.

"Good morning, John," I called gaily as he entered the gate and came toward the spot where I knelt on the newly turned ground.

"Mornin', Fee." Something in his voice made me look at him more closely. His lined face was drawn, his eyes shadowed, and in his hand, he clutched a familiar-looking paper. My stomach dropped. Once before, he had entered my yard with a telegram in his hand.

Six years ago, the telegram from my sister informed me of her marriage to the man I loved. Other than my telegram telling her of our father's death nearly a year later, and her reply that she would be unable to attend his funeral, it had been the last communication between us. I doubted this one held any better tidings.

I got to my feet, wiped my hands on my apron, and straightened the kerchief that covered my thick black hair before reaching for the parchment.

"Fee," he murmured, but I cut him off.

"Is it from Desi?" I asked, trying to hide the quaver of my voice. Perhaps I already knew what it would say. All my life, I had heard tales of twins who knew each other's pain or read each other's minds, but Desdemona and I had always been too busy cultivating our differences to pay much attention to our similarities. At some point in time, those differences seemed to have severed any ties that might once have bound us. Now, a hollow pit formed in my stomach as I held out my hand. "Give it to me."

He placed it in my palm, his strong old fingers

closing around mine for just a moment. He said my name again, and I shook my head in denial of the sympathy his voice held.

Tears clouded my vision as I stared down at the three words that separated my sister and me forever.

Desdemona is dead.

"How?" I whispered. "What happened to her?"

"I don't know. I've sent a telegram back, asking for more information about her death, as well as when the funeral will be held. As soon as I hear from them, I'll come around to tell you what I've learned. I'm sorry, Fee. I know how much you loved her. How close the two of you were."

Were. What a horrible word to describe my relationship with my sister, a painful reminder that everything between us had suddenly become past tense.

"Thank you, John. Would you have Amos make travel arrangements for me to leave as early in the morning as possible?"

"Of course. Would you like to come out to the house with me? Jess will be happy for the company, and it would keep you from being alone. Or I could take you up to Mrs. Dupree's house, if you'd rather."

His wife, Jess, was a kind woman and the closest thing to an aunt I had ever known. She would cluck and fuss over me, insisting I allow her to coddle me through my shock and grief. Adelaide Dupree, who was more grandmother than aunt and had taken Desi and me in hand when our father would have allowed us to run wild, would feed me until I could barely walk while she lectured me on mourning etiquette and regaled me with stories of the many people she had lived to mourn in her lifetime. My nerves were simply too exposed for such ministrations at the moment, however, and I shook my head.

"No, but thank you. I need to pack and prepare the house for my departure. I will let you know right away if I need anything," I assured him when he looked as if he might protest.

He looked doubtful but accepted my assurance without argument. With a pat on my arm and another murmured condolence, he was gone, leaving me alone with my grief and regret.

My bags were packed and I was pacing the tiny living room of my childhood home when he came again. What he brought was news that seemed to connect me to my sister in a way nothing had done in the last six years. As certainly as I knew that it was my face that stared back at me in the mirror each morning, I knew the words he spoke were untrue.

Our love for the same man may have ripped us apart, but in that moment, our mutual love for him brought Desdemona and me back together.

Even as John Bailey told me the sparse details he'd learned of her death, I heard Desi whisper a denial. Cade Scott might be any number of things, but a murderer he was not.

Chapter Two

I arrived at Almenara just before dusk the next evening. In the fading light, I could see the stone lighthouse Cade had described to me long ago. Built years before the main house, it was the beacon that gave the plantation its Spanish name.

My first thought as we crested the small hill that hid Cade's ancestral home from the main road was that it was far too innocent-looking a place to be the site of Desdemona's murder. A large house built of white stone, with pillars supporting the porch, black shutters framing the windows, and well-tended cotton fields lining the gravel drive, it was difficult to believe it housed someone evil enough to kill. My sister was dead, however, and as we rushed up the drive, a mist rolled in from the ocean, nearly obscuring the house and the fields from view. Leaning closer to the window, I scanned each shadowed face we passed, wondering if it was the face of a killer.

When we at last came to a stop in the wide paved drive in front of the house, I alighted, ignoring the shocked gasp of the young man who helped me down, just as I had the wide-eyed surprise of the man who picked me up from the station and brought me here.

It was impossible to ignore the horror of the petite, dark-haired maid who pulled the door open at my knock, however. Before I could speak a word, she let loose a bloodcurdling scream and crumpled to the ground.

Within seconds, there were at least a dozen servants gaping at me as I knelt beside the girl slowly regaining her senses. As soon as her eyes opened, she shot upright, scrambling away from me in a panic. At last, a woman in the black, high-necked uniform of a housekeeper stepped forward.

"Good evening, miss. May I help you?" Years of keeping a gaggle of young maids in line worked to keep her voice steady, but beneath her cool demeanor her face was pale and her gray eyes puzzled.

"I am Ophelia Garrett. Desdemona Scott was my sister." I stood up, holding my hand out to her as I did so.

A sigh of relief rippled through the room, and the rigid shoulders of the housekeeper relaxed.

"Miss Garrett," she said, taking my hand in hers, "please forgive our surprise. We had no idea Mrs. Scott had a sister."

As was her custom, Desdemona had left me behind and never looked back. I must admit it stung a bit to think that no one here had known of my existence.

"Fee?" No one except him, I corrected myself, turning at the sound of Cade's low, familiar voice. He stood above us, looking down on the foyer from the upstairs landing.

In the years since Cade married my sister, I had tried to convince myself that the handsome young man I remembered was somewhat embellished by my own fertile imagination. As he stood before me now, partially illuminated by the dimming light from the window behind him, I knew I was wrong. If anything, my memories were duller than reality. Eyes dark as night swept over me, and I felt my breath catch in my throat as his burning gaze came to rest on my face. The years seemed to slip away, and for a moment we were young again and free of regret. I could almost smell the jasmine that bloomed along the riverbank where we had walked hand in hand, hear the cries of the street vendors and the gentle splash of the oars in the water. For one long moment, I could almost taste his kiss.

I tore my gaze away from his and forced myself to stand straighter. He was my sister's husband, after all, and I could not and would not allow myself to give in to the attraction I had once felt for him.

"I'm so sorry to hear about Desdemona, Cade," I said, a bit surprised at the normality of my voice and by my stilted words.

"As am I, Ophelia," he said, once more the self-assured master of Almenara. His lips curled into a mocking imitation of the smile I remembered, and his eyes hardened to obsidian ice. He came down the stairs toward me, greeting me with a cold, quick embrace. "I hated the impersonal means of alerting you to your sister's death, but there was no other way. As I'm sure you've been told, I am not free to leave Almenara at this time."

A murmur of disapproval followed his announcement, reminding me of the servants still grouped about us, studying me with open curiosity.

"Could we speak privately, please?" I asked, the coldness of my voice matching his. "I have a great number of questions."

"Yes, of course. Follow me." To the housekeeper, he said, "Mrs. Hartley, please bring a pot of tea to my

7

study momentarily."

I followed him down the wide, shadowed hallway, glancing into the dark rooms on either side as we passed.

A cry of distress escaped me as we came to a room that was obviously a ballroom. Black velvet shrouded the mirrors lining the walls, but candlelight glinted off the gold trim and cast a peaceful glow across the polished oak of the casket containing my sister's earthly remains.

I wasn't sure why Cade thought we could walk past without him even mentioning the fact that Desi rested there, but I could see that he had.

"Let's talk first, Fee," he suggested softly, reaching for my arm when he realized I intended to enter the room. "There are things you should know at once."

I rejected his words and impatience as I shook off his hand and crossed the polished parquet floor to stand beside the coffin. The lid was closed and locked, and a large portrait of Desdemona rested on a flower-covered table beside the casket. Shining blue eyes, raven hair, and the aura that lured men to her like flies were so evident in the portrait, it was as if she were standing before me. Remorse filled me, and, for the first time since John Bailey handed me the letter informing me of her death, sobs overtook me.

I felt Cade come to stand behind me, and I fought the urge to fling myself against him, to feel comforting arms about me as I cried.

"Ophelia," he said, placing a large hand on my shoulder.

I swung around to face him.

"What happened to her, Cade?" I cried out, all the

forced haughtiness of moments before gone as we faced each other.

"Come. We can't talk here."

He wrapped his arm around my shoulder and led me from the room. After passing several closed doors, he ushered me into a large masculine study, pointed me to a leather upholstered chair, and took his seat behind the mahogany desk in front of the window.

I dabbed my eyes, trying to get hold of my emotions and concentrate on the explanation I felt certain Cade was about to offer.

He pinched the bridge of his nose, a gesture I remembered quite well from the time I'd known him. "What did they tell you?"

"They told me she was gone," I said, reluctant to say more. Surely he knew the rest of the message that had been delivered back to us in answer to John's questions.

He lifted his gaze to mine, inviting the whole of what I'd been told. Although the details had been few, the gist of them was unmistakable.

"They said you murdered her, but I can't believe that."

His dark eyes delved the depth of mine, as if searching for the truth of my words.

"Tell me how she died," I insisted softly. "Please."

He was silent for so long I began to wonder if he intended to say anything at all. Finally, he motioned toward the window behind his desk.

"When it's daylight, you can see from here the old lighthouse overlooking the bay. You would have had a good view of it from the main road before the fog rolled in, even at dusk. My great-grandparents moved here a hundred years ago to tend it and built the plantation while doing so. The lighthouse hasn't been used in years, and it's nearly invisible on a moonless night like tonight. Desdemona went there every day. Her body was found on the rocks below, three days ago."

I stared at him, trying to gauge his frame of mind and the reason for such dispassionate words to describe Desdemona's death. Certainly he was just as overcome with grief and shock as I was. Surely he was heartbroken at the loss of his wife.

At home, I had been so certain he was innocent, but faced with his lack of emotion as he recounted these minimal details of her death, I felt the first stirring of doubt. It had been years since I had seen him, and even though I had once imagined myself in love with him, I hardly knew him at all.

I met Cade in New Orleans when I was enlisted to be the summer traveling companion of Mrs. Dupree. Cade had been visiting the city with a small group of schoolmates celebrating their graduation from university. As luck would have it, we were all guests at the same hotel, along with mutual acquaintances of Mrs. Dupree and Cade's late parents. The older couple introduced me to Cade the night we arrived in town, and as young love often is, ours was instantaneous and all-consuming. With Mrs. Dupree's approval, Cade courted me throughout my stay, and had I not been called home suddenly to care for my father, Cade and I would have been engaged by the time we left New Orleans at the end of the summer. As it turned out, however, I was called home the week after my sister's arrival in New Orleans, and I never saw Cade again until I stood in the foyer of Almenara. I never saw Desi again at all.

I gave myself a mental shake, and in a voice that quavered much less than I expected, prodded him to continue. Certainly there were more details to be had.

"She fell?"

"No, there's little doubt she was forced over the railing."

I made a small sound of denial. "How can you be so sure? Who would do such a thing?"

He gave a bitter bark of laughter. "Apparently, I would."

"I don't believe that."

"Really? And why is that, Ophelia?" he asked dryly, leaning back in his chair as if he couldn't care less what I was about to say. The young man I had known had not been prone to such mocking cynicism, and I wondered what had turned him into the calloused man he appeared to be, or if it was perhaps his grief and shock that made him appear that way.

"I don't know," I admitted. "I just can't believe it."

"Well that will stand up beautifully in court."

"Court?"

"Yes, court. When they arrest me, I'll stand trial for murder."

"When they arrest you? Not if?"

He shook his head. "No, not if, Fee. They'll be here any minute."

My head was spinning, and I pressed my fingertips to my temples. What did he mean?

"They're convinced I'm guilty, even if you aren't. The sheriff wanted to take me in sooner, but I persuaded him to wait until you arrived."

I stared at him blankly, wondering why he would

have done such a thing, and why the local law enforcement would have agreed to it if they were convinced of his guilt.

"Arresting and physically taking me in is just a formality, Fee. I should be home by tomorrow night. Everyone knows I won't leave Almenara. I'll be here when it's time for the trial." He leaned forward, dark eyes burning with anxiety. "There are things I need to tell you first. We need to make arrangements for Tabby."

"Tabby?" I repeated the name in confusion.

A furrow appeared in his brow and I could see my confusion surprised him. Before he could explain, I heard the sound of booted feet in the hallway. He seemed to pale a bit beneath his tan, and I instinctively reached for his hand. Before I touched him, he jerked it away and surged to his feet.

The door burst open and two men entered the room. The younger of the two, tall and wiry, with blond hair and worried green eyes, stepped toward the desk.

"We're here to bring you in, Cade. I'm sorry we couldn't wait longer, but Calvin was anxious to get it done." He tipped his hat at me. "I'm sorry to interrupt, ma'am."

"Dennis, this is my sister-in-law, Ophelia. Fee, Dennis Ames. He'll be investigating Desdemona's death."

I doubted Cade's obvious cut to the older, larger man went unnoticed by anyone in the room, and as I shook Dennis Ames' hand, the bearded bear of a man stepped forward. In spite of his size and the anger that rolled from him in great waves, he was an unmistakably handsome man.

"Sheriff Calvin Scott," he said, holding out his hand. "I'll be leading the investigation into your sister's death. If my cousin chooses to ignore that fact, it will be his folly."

Cade grunted his opinion of the thinly veiled threat.

"This is obviously a mistake, Mr. Scott," I declared, my hand still caught in his. "Cade couldn't have killed my sister. You must know that."

"I knew Desdemona well, Miss Garrett, and I know Cade. I can assure you that he is the only person who is a suspect in her murder, the only person with any motive at all."

"Motive?" I repeated in surprise. "What motive?"

The man looked at Cade through dark, hooded eyes, watching for a reaction. When none was forthcoming, he sighed in barely concealed exasperation and turned back to me. His dark gaze shone with appreciation as it ran the length of my body, before returning to my face, which I felt heat with embarrassment.

"Desdemona was an extremely beautiful woman, as are you. She was a friendly sort, and I'm looking forward to learning just how similar you are in ways other than appearance."

The reaction he'd obviously been trying to garner from Cade was instantaneous and so violent I fell back against the desk with a cry of alarm.

Cade pushed his cousin against the wall, his arm pressing across Calvin's throat.

"Don't you dare touch her," Cade ground out, his face inches from the other man's.

"I've never been a man who had to initiate the touching," Calvin sneered. "I doubt that's going to change now."

Cade's fist connected with his nose in a devastating blow. Dennis Ames was on Cade in an instant, but there was no need for him to be. As soon as his cousin sank to the floor, Cade seemed to deflate.

"Let's get this over with, Dennis," he said wearily and let the younger man handcuff him without further incident.

He lifted his eyes to mine, and I couldn't mistake the banked fury in their ebony depths.

"Do you still believe I couldn't have killed her?" he asked.

I knew he expected his violent outburst to have changed my opinion, and even though I had questioned his innocence only moments before, I didn't give my answer an ounce of thought.

"Yes."

Chapter Three

I followed Cade and Dennis down the hall, past the room where my sister was enclosed in the glossy wood coffin, and through the front door I'd entered barely an hour before.

"Excuse us, miss," a man's voice said from behind me, and I stepped out of the way of two young, brawny grooms who hefted Calvin's limp form between them. Blood trickled from his nose and, as they passed, one crimson drop hit the floor at my feet.

For a moment, it all seemed too much, and I fought a wave of dizziness that caused me to sway where I stood.

"Don't do it, Cade!" Dennis shouted from what seemed a mighty distance.

"See to her, then, damn it!" Cade's roar cleared some of the fuzz from my brain, and I looked up to see Dennis hurrying toward me as Cade fought against the men who held him in place beside the deputy's wagon. Dennis's arm encircled my waist and he led me back inside the house.

Mrs. Hartley met us in the foyer, tea tray in hand, and I wondered if she could really have missed the uproar of the officers' arrival and Cade's arrest. With a gasp, she set the tray on a table and took Dennis's place at my side, guiding me to a room off the nearest corridor.

"I'm fine," I insisted, but Mrs. Hartley just clucked kindly.

"It's been a trying day for you, dear. You just need a little rest and refreshment."

"I'll check on you later, Ophelia," Dennis said. He blushed sheepishly. "I mean, Miss Garrett. I've heard so much about you, I feel like I already know you."

"Ophelia is fine. Fee is even better," I told him. "My father, bless his soul, gave Desi and me both nicknames as soon as he recorded the names our mother assigned us."

"Quite good of him," Mrs. Hartley said as she pushed me gently into a chair.

I became aware of the tears on my cheeks only when the woman pressed a handkerchief into my hand and hurried from the room to retrieve the tea from the hall table.

I dabbed at my eyes, scanning the airy room around me. Where Cade's study had been decorated with dark wood and leather furniture, this one was decorated with white walls and soft shades of blue and yellow that dispelled the darkness outside its windows and walls. A large painting hung above the mantel, and I knew without asking that it had belonged to my sister. The artist had caught a bird in flight as it circled over a vast expanse of sand and rock I felt oddly certain looked exactly like the place where she died. The fact that the artist had quite definitely been looking down at the bird made me think it had been painted from the top of the lighthouse. Wherever he had been, he had managed to catch the very essence of Desi's love of soaring birds.

"This was Mrs. Scott's morning room," Mrs.

16

Hartley informed me as she entered with the tray of tea and iced cakes. She looked around and her eyes settled on the picture. "She did love the birds, you know. She would sit up in the lighthouse all day watching them fly."

"She always did love them," I agreed as she bent to fill my cup with tea. "Did she have the picture painted?"

"Oh, yes, miss. She commissioned a gentleman from up north to paint it. Devlin was his name. Quite the ladies' man, he was. All the girls were head over heels for him." As if remembering her place and mine in the household, she straightened and stepped away. "I'll just be seeing to supper, then. It's being served a bit late tonight."

"There's no need to serve it formally on my account, Mrs. Hartley. I'll be happy to eat in my room, or even the kitchen if you and the others will have me."

She looked at me oddly. "That won't be necessary, of course. Miss Eleanor, Mr. Calvin, and Mrs. Lorraine must dine as usual. You will join them in the dining room, unless you prefer the solace of your room for tonight."

"I'm sorry, Mrs. Hartley. I have no idea who those people are." At her look of surprise, I sighed. "My sister and I hadn't spoken in nearly six years."

"Oh, dear," she gasped. "Well, you've already met Mr. Calvin, of course. Lorraine is his wife and Eleanor is his sister."

"Calvin? The man who came to arrest Cade? He lives here?" I was shocked when she nodded her head. How could two men with such obvious animosity as Cade and Calvin Scott live under the same roof? What

17

kind of household could withstand the violent dislike that simmered between them?

"Oh, yes. Mr. Cade has lived here all his life. He was not quite a year old when his mother died, and he and his father moved to Almenara. Mr. Calvin and Miss Eleanor were born and raised near Charleston. Their father was killed at Appomattox, and there was no word of them or their mother for several years afterward. The elder Mr. Scott was about to go out of his mind with worry when they finally showed up on the doorstep. I declare, miss, a more ragtag bunch you've never seen. Mr. Calvin was ten by that time, Miss Eleanor was six, and Mr. Cade had just turned five. Mr. Cade was as fine a little gentleman as you've ever seen, but the others? Well, they'd had a hard lot of it since their daddy died, and they arrived as dirty and starved as you can imagine. Sad to see, but they straightened out quick enough. Now you can't tell which ones were raised here from the get-go and which ones weren't."

"And they've all continued to live here together all these years?"

"Of course, miss. I believe their grandfather set things up so that Miss Eleanor and Mr. Calvin would always have a home at Almenara, although Mr. Cade inherited it after his father's and grandfather's deaths. The house is certainly big enough to house them all."

I wondered if any house was that accommodating, but I could hardly say so to the housekeeper.

"Miss Garrett," she began hesitantly, as if unsure how to say what she wanted to say. "Before he was taken away, did Mr. Cade happen to mention Miss Tabitha?"

"Tabitha?"

"Your sister's daughter."

Desdemona had a child? A daughter she'd named after our late mother?

Somewhere deep in my heart, I'd always hoped, prayed even, that when it came time for us to be mothers, when I had found someone to ease my aching loneliness and make my love for Cade seem like nothing more than the summer infatuation I tried to convince myself it was, my sister and I would be friends once more. Countless times I had stared out over the fields where Desi and I had once run wild, and imagined raven-haired children playing there, their laughter echoing through the yard of our father's home. I had let myself believe that we had time to forgive and live as sisters once more.

Now I knew how wrong I had been. Time had run out, Desi was dead, and even when she'd been alive and given birth to a child of her own, she had kept it a secret from me.

"You didn't know?" Her decorum forgotten, the housekeeper sat beside me, resting a soft, sympathetic hand on my back. "The child is already down for the night, and I suspect you're worn out from your travel and all the excitement. If you'd like, I'll have a maid bring a supper tray to your room. After a good night's rest, you can meet Miss Tabitha first thing in the morning."

I would have preferred not to wait until morning, but I understood the need to conform to the child's schedule, and I hated to wake her if she was already asleep.

"Do you think it will upset her when she sees me looking so much like her mother?"

"I don't think you need to worry about her being confused. I think perhaps it is only at first glance that you look so much like Mrs. Scott. Below the surface, there appears to be something quite different, and that is what Tabitha will see."

I hoped she was right. Most people didn't notice the differences between us, but they were there nonetheless, and to anyone more than a casual onlooker, they were probably startlingly obvious. As Calvin Scott had said, Desi was beautiful, and I had enough sense to deduce that since we were nearly identical, I could hardly be considered plain. Unlike my sister, however, I had attracted only one man in this lifetime. Unfortunately for me, when I left his side to care for our ailing father, I was quickly and easily replaced by my dear sister.

The fact that the memory could still cause me pain was reason enough for me to have stayed away from Almenara.

****

The large bedroom Mrs. Hartley assigned to me was lovely, with pink cabbage roses on the wallpaper and a sleigh bed covered in a matching quilt. A small table and two chairs sat before bow windows which, according to Mrs. Hartley, overlooked the flower gardens below.

I was sitting there an hour later when there was a light knock on the door, and a maid entered carrying a tray of steaming food. I quickly removed my journal and pens from the table so that she could set the tray there.

"Good evening, miss," the girl said, her eyes avoiding mine as she put the tray down and hurried for the door.

As soon as the door clicked shut, I heard the sound of her footsteps running for the stairs. Obviously, the staff had yet to overcome the shock of my arrival, and I wondered if, by the time I returned home next week, they would be any less inclined to look at me as if I were the ghost of their late mistress.

I enjoyed the steaming plate of well-flavored roast and potatoes, bathed away the dust of my journey, and crawled into bed. I was asleep within moments, and slept soundly through the night, except for several times when the wind wailing outside my window roused me to semi-awareness. Storms had never frightened or disturbed me, so I paid it little attention as I rolled over and slept again.

Chapter Four

I woke early the next morning and went to the windows to survey the garden Mrs. Hartley had told me about. I expected to see some slight wind damage and puddles from the night's storm. The ground was dry, however, and there wasn't a blade of grass or a limb out of place in the beautifully landscaped flower garden.

A gardener knelt beside a raised-bed garden filled with blooming mums and orange asters. As if feeling my gaze on him, he turned and looked up at my window, his hand shading his eyes. He stood to his feet, his eyes never leaving my window, as he crossed himself and backed away. He disappeared somewhere past the gate that led around the side of the house, and I imagined him running, anxious to tell everyone he had seen Desdemona's ghost.

I pulled an unadorned black crepe dress from my case and dressed with some care. I would meet my young niece for the first time today, and I was quite certain I would not be able to avoid meeting Cade's relatives for much longer. Our father had drilled into our heads the importance of first impressions, and as I looked in the full-length mirror standing between the lavatory door and the fireplace, I was satisfied with the impression I would give. No one would mistake me for a socialite, with my plain, unassuming attire and carefully arranged chignon. Neither would they mistake me for a pauper, for my dress was of a good quality for a woman of my station. I was, after all, not an inhabitant of Almenara, but the orphaned daughter of a modest and frugal country vicar.

Mrs. Hartley arrived with a breakfast tray just as I finished my morning prayers and devotional, and we agreed I would ring for her once I had eaten.

I was so excited at the thought of meeting Tabitha I barely tasted my food and was done in short order.

"I'm surprised there wasn't some damage from the storm last night," I observed as Mrs. Hartley and I passed the wall of windows in the long corridor outside my door. The windows opened onto a wide veranda that looked out over a courtyard and the pebbled paths leading down to the shore.

Mrs. Hartley shook her head. "There wasn't a storm last night, miss."

"Of course there was. Didn't you hear the wind howling about outside?"

She gave me a strange look, and shook her head. "I didn't hear a peep of it."

"Oh. Perhaps I was dreaming then." I knew I hadn't dreamed the wailing of the wind, but I didn't argue the point. Perhaps she was a heavier sleeper than I was, or perhaps her room let in less sound.

"Yes, you were probably overexcited by the events of the day."

She grew quiet as we continued down the hall, turning twice until we were in the corridor of the wing that ran parallel to mine. This wing was darker, the sun that should have come through the veranda windows blocked by heavy brocade curtains. We passed two doors before she stopped, turning toward me with knitted brow.

"Miss Garrett, I want to prepare you to meet Miss Tabitha, but I'm not sure of the appropriate words with which to do so. She is a very special child, and your sister loved her dearly, of course. But I'm afraid Mrs. Scott found it somewhat difficult to come to terms with her oddities. Perhaps that is why she put off informing you of the child's existence."

"Oddities?" I repeated, struck by the use of such a word in the description of a child.

"For lack of a better word, yes. She is five years old, a tiny little thing, and although bright and sharp as a tack in some ways, dreadfully slow in others. She doesn't walk well, doesn't talk at all, and according to the doctors may never do the things most children her age can do."

I tried not to let my dismay at her description show as I straightened my spine and motioned toward the nursery. "I'm sure my niece and I will get along quite well, Mrs. Hartley. I can hardly wait to meet her."

Long ago, our father had taken Desi and me to visit the home of one of his colleagues. Reverend Dawson's son was a twenty-six-year-old man with the mind of a child. Though he had been nearly two decades older than we were at the time, my sister and I had sat on the ground beside him, building castles out of colorful wooden blocks and guarding them with his precious collection of toy soldiers. A vivid memory of that summer afternoon came to me now as I stared into the flattened face and bright, almond-shaped eyes of my niece.

"Hello, Tabby, I'm your Aunt Fee," I said, kneeling before her. She wore a blue dress that matched her eyes, and a wide red scarf secured her in her seat. She grunted what I took to be a greeting as she banged her hands excitedly against the arms of the rocking chair. I wondered if perhaps she thought I was her mother, or if she understood I was not.

"I was just feeding her, miss," the young maid who sat on the floor beside her told me. I was impressed with how quickly Mrs. Hartley had gotten the maids in order as the girl quickly quelled the spark of unease in her eyes, which I was sure was caused by my presence. "She loves to eat."

"And what are you eating?" I asked Tabitha, as she grunted at the maid.

"Porridge, miss." The maid leaned toward me as she spooned some into Tabby's mouth. "She doesn't talk, you know."

"Yes, I know." I smiled wistfully. "That could be something of a blessing for you. Her mother talked so much, when we were her age, I thought our father would go mad. At times he resorted to stuffing cotton in his ears just to get some peace and quiet."

The maid giggled, then clasped a hand against her mouth as if remembering this was a house of mourning.

Tears welled in my eyes when I thought of Desi trailing behind my father as he worked in the garden, cotton sticking out from his ears like stuffing from a well-used rag doll.

If he had listened more, would she have stayed close to us? It was the first time I had ever wondered what part my father played in Desi's follies, and I felt disloyal as soon as the thought entered my mind.

Tabitha made a trilling sound with her tongue, bringing my focus back to her, and I smiled through my tears. This child was my family now, the last remaining relative I had, and she needed me as no one had in many, many years.

I had come to Almenara to say goodbye to my sister and to find answers to my questions about her death. When I left home, I had expected it would all be sorted out quickly and I would be home again within a week, but between Cade's arrest and Tabitha's existence, I suspected I would be here much longer than anticipated.

I stayed in the nursery, getting to know my niece and her routine, for several hours, finally making my way downstairs when her nursemaid, Janie, put her down for an afternoon nap. I was searching for Mrs. Hartley, following the same hall Cade and I had taken the day before, and I slowed as I neared the room where my sister lay.

I could no more pass it by than I could change the color of the sky, so I walked toward the casket, my eyes focused on the portrait of Desi.

"Oh, Desi," I sighed as I picked the portrait up and ran my fingers over the image of her beloved face. "What happened to you?"

"That is the question of the day, is it not?"

Startled, I spun around, the frame falling from my hands and shattering on the floor at my feet.

"Forgive me for frightening you, Miss Garrett," a lovely, statuesque blonde said as she crossed the room to the bell pull. The red and white dress she wore was low cut, with a small matching cap that rested atop her curls. "I thought perhaps you heard me approaching."

"No, I'm afraid I didn't."

"One of the maids will do that." She waved her

hand in dismissal as I bent to pick up the frame, and before I could straighten with it in my hand, a maid appeared. She genuflected before entering the room, saw the glass, and hurried away, presumably to retrieve a broom and dustpan.

"The help at Almenara are a superstitious lot," the blonde drawled, her hands resting on her shapely hips. "Most of them refuse to enter this room at all. They've always been so certain the house is haunted. Now, more than ever. As if Desdemona would still be here now that she's finally free of this godforsaken place."

"Lorraine?" A female voice sounded from the hallway, and the woman turned toward the door. I tried to remember the names of the family Mrs. Hartley had given me the night before and settled on Lorraine as Calvin's wife.

"Yes, Eleanor?" Impatience tempered the woman's voice.

"Have you found her yet? I checked the nursery, but she isn't there, and Janie claims to have no idea where she might be."

A pretty, rather plump brunette in a morning dress of royal blue stopped talking as she appeared in the doorway, and after a brief moment of perusal, hurried toward me, embracing me warmly.

"Miss Garrett, it is so nice to finally meet you."

"I'm sorry, but you both seem to have me at quite a disadvantage," I told her, still clutching the picture in my hands.

"Oh, no, don't tell me Lorraine didn't have the courtesy to introduce herself."

"I hardly had time, Eleanor. You found us quite soon after I entered the room."

Eleanor chuckled and waved her hand toward Lorraine. "I am Eleanor Scott, and this is my sister-in-law, the highly esteemed Lorraine Walden Scott."

I gasped involuntarily and Lorraine gave a brittle laugh. "So you recognize me now, do you? Lorraine Walden, stage actress extraordinaire. Hardly highly esteemed, as Eleanor puts it, but well known all the same. Although, to be fair, it was for talents unrelated to the theater."

A decade before, Lorraine Walden's affair with a prominent judge had spread through the newspapers like wildfire. My father had hidden the daily paper for weeks, trying to keep the worst of the innuendos and gossip from our impressionable prying eyes. He hadn't been a huge success, however, as we'd found where he stashed them and snuck them into our room, where we regaled each other and our friends with dramatic and emotional readings of the endless updates. My father might never have known had it not been for one particularly melodramatic rendition that sent us into fits of giggling that woke him and brought him to our room. Had Desi remembered that incident when she met Lorraine for the first time?

I could feel Lorraine's hard stare, and I gave myself a mental shake. My father would be as appalled by my rudeness as he had been by our secret readings.

"It's my pleasure to meet you, Mrs. Scott, and you, Miss Scott."

Eleanor laughed. "Oh, please, you must call us by our given names. If we stood on such formality, we'd never know who anyone was talking to. Not with three of us having the same surname." She cringed and tears welled in her eyes. "Two now. I'm so sorry, Miss

28

Garrett."

"Call me Fee, please," I told her.

"Fee?" Lorraine repeated. "What an odd name."

"It's short for Ophelia."

"Ophelia and Desdemona? Othello and Hamlet?" Lorraine seemed amused and Eleanor unfazed by the connotations of our names.

I was saved from any further explanation by the sound of masculine voices outside the room. I recognized Cade's voice immediately and, still clutching the picture of my sister in my hand, I rushed into the hall.

"Cade!" I stopped myself just short of throwing my arms around him. "You're free."

"Not really. I'm just no longer being housed at the jail. My cousin and I reached an agreement," he said, without elaborating, but Calvin Scott's smug smile let me know it wasn't an agreement that sat well with Cade.

"An agreement?" Even without turning to look at her, I sensed Lorraine's barely controlled excitement as she spoke.

"Yes, my love, an agreement that allows Cade to be home with his child yet assures the townspeople that a dangerous criminal is under the control of local authority." Calvin stepped around me and offered his arm to his wife.

Lorraine practically purred as she moved to his side, and with Eleanor following quietly in their wake, they turned the corner at the far end of the hall.

Cade and I faced each other awkwardly. I couldn't lie to myself and say that my attraction to him had lessened over time. Even with the deepening lines of worry around his eyes and the dark changes I sensed in him, I found him to be heartbreakingly handsome.

His gaze swept over me, and I thought he looked almost relieved when his eyes settled on the picture in my hand. Was he as glad as I that he found something else to catch his attention?

"You're bleeding, Fee." He took my wrist and lifted my hand for a better view of my wound.

I hadn't realized I was grasping the frame so hard that a small shard of glass had sliced the length of my thumb.

Cade gently removed the frame from my hand and set it on the ornate table beside us. He pulled a handkerchief from his pocket and blotted at my thumb. This required me to move somewhat closer to him, and I breathed in the masculine scent of him as he bent his head to study the cut.

"It doesn't look like there's any glass left in it. Does it hurt?"

"No. It's fine." My voice sounded breathless, and I felt heat rise up in my face. I pulled my hand away from his but couldn't quite bring myself to step away from him. I forced myself to remember why I was here. My sister was dead, and I had learned almost nothing about her death since my arrival. "How did Desi die, Cade?"

He lifted his head, his face mere inches from mine. Emotion clouded his gaze, and he opened his mouth as if he meant to answer me. Instead, a low moan escaped him and he caught my mouth in the hungry kiss I had dreamed of for six years' worth of lonely nights. For just a moment, the reason for that loneliness was completely forgotten.

A cry rent the air, and I jerked away from Cade, guilt and alarm whipping through me in equal measures as I turned to stare at the maid who had finally returned with the broom and dustpan.

"Oh, Mr. Scott, forgive me, please."

"No need for apologies, Susan," Cade said, bringing the woman's stammering apology to an end. He looked at me, his eyes shadowed with pain. "I'm the one who should be sorry. I'll see you at supper, Ophelia."

I was left standing in the hall with the maid, who stared at me with open disdain. Her voice was sharp and cold when she spoke.

"I thought you were Mrs. Scott, you know. Kissing her husband like that. It made me think Kathleen was right and she had come back from the grave after all."

"People don't come back from the grave, Susan," I retorted, hoping my haughtiness hid my shame. If Desi were to come back to haunt the halls of the home where she'd died, I was fairly certain what I'd just done would be reason enough for me to be her target.

Chapter Five

I was still reeling from Cade's kiss and my own wildly guilty conscience when a knock on my bedroom door announced the arrival of Mrs. Hartley and a pretty red-haired maid I guessed to be a year or so younger than I.

"Miss Garrett, this is Dory. She will act as your lady's maid during your stay at Almenara."

Having lived alone for the better part of five years, and with only my father for the year prior to that, the thought of having a lady's maid was somewhat ludicrous.

"That's really not necessary, Mrs. Hartley," I protested. "I'm quite used to taking care of myself."

"And everyone else," Cade said as he came through the door. The three of us looked at him in surprise. It was far from acceptable for him to enter my room, but he waved away our silent disapproval. "I haven't come here for any nefarious purpose, ladies. I saw Mrs. Hartley and Dory coming up the stairs and suspected you'd have some objection to having a maid. So I followed them, hoping I could talk you into going along."

"Cade, you know I have no use for a maid."

"When I met you, you had a lady's maid."

"When you met me, I was a different girl." I hoped it wasn't bitterness that made my voice sound so sharp.

His dark eyes searched mine, wistfulness and regret so evident I was certain the other two women could see. I knew he was remembering the girl I had been at nineteen. Only half a decade separated me from that girl, yet I felt as if I were centuries away from her.

"She wasn't my maid," I continued. "She worked for Mrs. Dupree."

He sighed and took my hands in his.

"Please, Fee. I know you aren't used to it, but it won't hurt you to be pampered a bit. Eleanor and Lorraine both dress quite elaborately for dinner."

"This is a house of mourning, Cade. Out of respect for Desi, there should be some downplay of fashion."

He dropped my hands and stepped away. His eyes turned cold, hard, and unfamiliar.

"I'm sorry, Ophelia, but you won't find much respect for your sister amongst those who live here. You may mourn her passing, but you do so alone."

With that shocking declaration, he turned and left the room.

I looked toward the two women who still stood beside me. A multitude of questions danced through my head, but I could hardly speak them to the housekeeper and the maid.

Taking a deep, fortifying breath, I motioned toward the wardrobe where someone, presumably Dory, had hung my clothes this morning.

"I have several appropriate dinner gowns, Dory. You can pick which one I wear. Then perhaps you could help me with my hair."

Following my lead, the housekeeper excused herself, shot a quick look of warning at Dory, and bid me call her should I need anything further.

As Dory went to the wardrobe to pick my dress, I took a seat at the dressing table and pulled the pins from my hair. She remained silent as she laid the dress across the bed and began to brush my long black tresses. As she brushed, I mulled over the day's events, especially Cade's kiss and his avowal that I was alone in mourning Desi's passing. Even if no one else in the house mourned her, shouldn't her husband have included himself in those who did?

A shiver rushed up my spine when I thought of Cade's dark, cold eyes. Could he really care as little as he seemed to?

"It isn't right, them not caring about Mrs. Scott being dead," Dory suddenly blurted out, the brush stopping in mid-stroke. She met my eyes in the mirror, and her voice dropped. "She's still here, for goodness' sake."

That was my sentiment exactly. Maybe none of the inhabitants of Almenara were heartbroken that she was dead, but with Desi's body still laid out in the ballroom, it seemed to me they should at least keep up some pretense of grief.

"Why don't they care?" I asked her, unconcerned that I was stepping over a line in discussing family business with a servant. I needed answers more than I needed to remain within society's bounds.

"Oh, miss, you can't imagine the way it was when she was alive. She and Mrs. Lorraine were always sniping at each other, and Mr. Calvin just leered at the both of them. Mr. Cade and him were always furious at each other. There's no love lost between any of them, as far as I can tell."

"But they are family." As if I were still foolish

enough to believe family couldn't hurt one another.

"My mama says Mr. Cade and Mr. Calvin have been fighting since the day they met each other. She says there's no one can hurt you as bad as those who know you best, and jealousy makes men pigheaded and blind."

I remained silent, battling my own need for answers. I reminded myself again that it simply wasn't acceptable for me to learn such things through the backstairs grapevine. Dory ignored my reticence as she continued.

"She says Mr. Calvin's always wanted what Mr. Cade had, and he's ate up with envy over Mr. Cade being the heir to Almenara instead of him. And having an acceptable wife, of course."

As the daughter of two second children who inherited nothing but the education and upbringing afforded the offspring of genteel parents, Desi wouldn't have been an acceptable wife for many wealthy households. At Almenara, however, where there were no longer any preceding generations alive to pull the strings of matrimony and future lineage, and where the only other wife was a former stage actress and infamous paramour, Desi must have been quite elevated in her acceptability.

I stood up and walked to the bed, my mind full of thoughts of Desi and how much she must have loved her place in this circle of the world. If there was one thing my sister had always dreamed of, it was to escape my father's modest way of life. I had often wondered in the years since she'd married Cade if she did so out of love for him or for the life he could offer her. I had always suspected that an equal mixture of the two drove her.

"Are you okay, miss?" Dory asked from beside me. She held a dress of midnight blue taffeta in her hands, and I pursed my lips, trying to keep them from trembling as I nodded.

"I'm fine."

She slipped the dress over my head and smoothed it down around my hips. "It's a very nice dress."

"Not quite black."

"It's close enough, I think."

She was right. It was very nearly black, the blue of it showing only in certain light, like a crow's wing. I had bought it in New Orleans, thinking I could wear it when accompanying my father in his bereavement duties, and I'd worn it to his funeral four years ago. I'd thought of Desi when I bought it, remembering a crow she'd nursed back to health when we were twelve, but I never dreamed I would wear it to mourn her death a few years later.

I quickly dashed away the threatening tears and took a deep breath as Dory stepped back and surveyed her handiwork.

"You look beautiful, miss."

"I'm in mourning, Dory. My looks don't matter."

"I think you are like your sister, Miss Garrett. Sadness makes you even prettier."

Startled by her words, I turned toward her. "Was she often sad?"

I watched Dory war with herself, wanting to tell me more but afraid to overstep her bounds.

I grasped her hands. "Please, Dory, tell me. What kind of life did my sister have here? Why was she sad? Who would have killed her?"

The questions poured out of me, and poor Dory looked as if she would love to run away, but I clung to her hands.

"Oh, miss, I really can't say." Her eyes darted to the doorway nervously.

"Please," I begged. "Please tell me what you know."

"That's enough, Ophelia."

I spun around at the sound of Cade's voice. He stood in the doorway, dressed for supper in a dark suit, his face a mask of cold fury.

"I deserve answers, Cade. Desi was my sister, and I want to know what happened to her."

"Dory, excuse us, please," he ground out, as he crossed the room toward me.

"But, Mister Cade—"

He cut off her protest with a slice of his hand in the air, pointing to the door, and she dashed from the room.

"I've told you what happened to Desdemona. She was murdered, thrown over the side of the lighthouse to the rocks below."

I shuddered at the thought. "Yes, you told me that, but you never told me who could have done it. Or why."

My voice broke on the last word, and his face softened.

"God knows you deserve the answers you're looking for, but I won't give them to you."

Mrs. Hartley appeared at the door, her anxious gaze relaxing when she caught sight of us.

"Miss Garrett?" she panted, making me wonder if she had run up the stairs. Had she been afraid for me being here with Cade alone? Had Dory told her he was angry? Had she feared he would harm me?

"Yes?" I answered, while Cade's words danced in my head. He hadn't said he couldn't tell me why Desdemona was murdered. Only that he wouldn't.

"I was given instructions to escort you downstairs once you were ready." Mrs. Hartley looked at Cade pointedly. "Right, sir?"

"Of course," he said with a slight incline of his head. He motioned toward the door. "After you, Ophelia."

With Cade trailing behind us, Mrs. Hartley led me to the parlor, where Cade's family was already gathered. The room was eerily silent, currents of emotion tangible beneath the surface, and all eyes turned to me as I entered. I have no idea where I found the resolve to meet them stare for stare.

Cade had been right about the lack of mourning attire I should expect. Eleanor had chosen to wear an orchid dress with deep purple trim at the sleeves and neckline, while Lorraine wore a bright emerald dinner dress with a diamond-studded brooch in the middle of her low-cut bodice.

After a few moments of intense scrutiny, Eleanor hurried toward me, slipping her arm in mine and ushering me into the room.

"You mustn't mind our rudeness, Fee. It is just still so strange to see you, looking so much like Desdemona and yet so different."

"Different?" Lorraine snorted.

"Of course," Eleanor said, "The differences are quite obvious, aren't they, Cade?"

She turned to Cade, and he nodded. "Yes, quite."

I blushed as Lorraine circled me, studying me from

every angle.

"The only difference I see is that this one might have a little class. If Ophelia were the one who had died, I sincerely doubt Desdemona would have wasted a perfectly good chance to show off her wares by wearing a mourning dress."

Appalled by her assessment of my sister, I spun to face her but was stilled by Cade's words.

"Absolutely correct, Lorraine, although I'm surprised that class was the difference you noticed."

Lorraine laughed, placing a hand to her chest as if her amusement was more than she could contain. "Cade, you bad, bad boy. I suppose you thought I'd notice, as you obviously did, that her wares are quite extraordinary compared to her sister's."

"Lorraine!" Eleanor trilled, the blush mottling her neck and cheeks testimony to her embarrassment at her sister-in-law's reference to my somewhat ample bosom. I fought a losing battle to hide it beneath the modest dresses I favored, and my hand went there of its own accord, resting on the blue-black fabric that covered me completely.

"I see now why it was so easy for you to comment on what you perceive as my sister's lack of class, Lorraine," I said coldly. "It must have been quite easy for you to recognize."

Lorraine pursed her lips until they turned white from the pressure. Her eyes sparked with anger and, for a moment, I expected her hand to meet my cheek. Instead, she smiled slowly and offered a little clap of her hands.

"Bravo, Ophelia," she applauded. "Well played."

"Dinner is served, sir," Mrs. Hartley said from the

doorway, and I breathed a sigh of relief as Cade took my arm and led me into the dining room. Calvin and Lorraine followed behind us, leaving Eleanor to bring up the rear alone.

I wondered what the others thought of Cade's solicitousness but then reminded myself that it was the appropriate thing for him to do. To the rest of the world, I was simply his sister-in-law, a houseguest come to mourn her sister's death at his side. They had no idea we had once been in love.

We were served a thick crab bisque, so flavorful a hum of appreciation nearly escaped me. Cade offered me a knowing smile as he spooned the soup into his own mouth, nearly causing me to choke. Could he possibly remember that just such a dish had been one of my favorites during our time in New Orleans?

I knew my face turned pink at the thought, and when I looked toward Eleanor and saw her staring at me, it must have turned a brilliant red.

"Cade," she said, turning her attention to him. "I'm quite sure that you and Desdemona came home to Almenara immediately after your marriage. Yet you and Ophelia seem quite familiar with one another. Did you stop off to meet Desdemona's family on your way home?"

I expected him to say yes, even though it was a lie, but he shook his head.

"No, I actually knew Fee before I met Desi. She was in New Orleans for a while before her sister arrived. Mr. and Mrs. Robertson introduced us."

"So were you there for the wedding?" Eleanor directed the question at me and I shook my head.

"No, I'm afraid I missed the wedding. Our father

was ill and I was called home to care for him."

"What of your sister? She wasn't needed at home?"

I saw the corner I had backed myself into. Speaking the truth, that my father refused to see his other daughter or forgive her for her transgressions, seemed disloyal and unfair to Desi. So I opened my mouth and, although it pained me to do so, spoke the lie that Desi and I had agreed upon when I left her behind in New Orleans.

"No, only one of us was needed at home. Desi was young and adventurous, with the future spread out before her, and I saw no reason for us both to return."

The truth was that Desdemona had been carrying on an affair with a married colleague of our father. When my father learned of it, he begged her to end the affair, but Desi refused. He had given her a ticket to join me and thrown her out of the house, hoping she would come to her senses and, if not repent of her sins, at least give up her lover. I always believed he intended for her to return home with me at the end of that summer, but when he had a stroke a week after her arrival in New Orleans, I returned alone. By that time, Desi was so ill and weak with worry over the whole sordid business, I feared for her health should she make the return trip so soon. We agreed that we would not risk the further upset her return might cause our father, and she took my place as Mrs. Dupree's companion while I boarded the train home alone. As Cade and Desi stood at the station, waving farewell, I never dreamed he would fall in love with her as soon as I disappeared from sight.

"You were twins, weren't you?" Lorraine's question interrupted my thoughts, and I looked over to find her studying me closely, as if she sensed my lies. "If she was of an age when her whole life was ahead of her, weren't you of that age as well?"

The servants cleared away the soup bowls and brought in the main course while everyone stared at me, awaiting my answer to Lorraine's question. Finally, when the servants had moved back to the kitchen, I shrugged.

"I suppose that's true. We were the same age, and I was young, still dreaming of a life other than the one I was given. But one of us had to go home, and I was the one we chose."

"How'd you do that? Draw straws? Flip a coin?" Calvin asked from his end of the table, his hooded eyes darting from me to Cade with interest.

My own eyes were drawn to Cade, who was staring at me as if he had never seen me before.

"You chose?" His voice was harsh and cold, slicing through me like a knife. "The both of you?"

"Yes. I had always been the one to help my father—"

"And to hell with the consequences?"

"It was the right choice," I assured him, determined to ignore the betrayal I detected in his questions. It wasn't I who had betrayed him, after all.

"For whom?"

"For everyone."

He shook his head in disbelief. "How could the two of you decide what was best for everyone?"

I was silent, and, as if sensing the tremulous state of my emotions, Eleanor began to fill her plate while prattling on about something as mundane as the saddle she was having made for her horse. She was interrupted

42

by Cade's hand meeting the table in fury. I jumped, dropping my butter knife and dinner roll on the table.

"Answer me, damn it!" Cade yelled as butter slid from my knife and pooled on the white linen tablecloth. "How did you and your sister decide who would stay and who would go?"

My eyes darted from Cade to the others, who all stared at him in slack-jawed surprise. "Cade, there isn't anything to say. I had to leave. My father needed me."

"Why you? Why not Desdemona?" he persisted.

Although my half-truths obviously upset him, I refused to speak ill of her by telling of my father's disowning her and his refusal to have her home. These people hated her, they didn't mourn for her, didn't care that she lay dead only a few rooms away. They only leaned forward in their chairs, anxious to hear the words that would justify their damnation of her.

"She wasn't well, and I was worried about her making the trip home. I doubted in her condition she would have been any help to my father."

He said nothing, simply stared at me with icy disdain that I imagined bordered on hatred.

Tears sprang to my eyes, and I stood quickly, upsetting my wine glass so that the bright red liquid spread in a puddle about the buttery mess I had already made.

"Excuse me," I whispered.

I rushed upstairs, where I threw myself across my bed and sobbed. I cried for Desdemona, the girl I once knew and the woman I never knew. I cried for my lost dreams of the future and all the futile hopes of reconciliation that I'd cherished all these years. I cried for her husband, who I still loved, and her child, who

I'd just discovered. And I cried for the truth I was coming to see.

For six years, I had tried unsuccessfully to convince myself that what Cade and I shared was nothing more than a youthful infatuation. I told myself that he and Desdemona were happy. I told myself that I had done the right thing and leaving them both behind had been for the best.

Now I knew better. Obviously something had gone horribly wrong here in this house. My sister had not found the peace and happiness she had grasped for all of her life, and Cade had not found the love I hoped he had. Instead they had lived a life that made it possible for him to be the prime suspect in her murder.

All this time, I had considered my loneliness a byproduct of my sister's happiness. Instead I was beginning to think it was just a result of my own careless manipulation of our lives and my stubborn refusal to take the first step toward reconciliation.

I eventually gained control of myself and got ready for bed. As I slipped between the sheets, I heard the murmured voices of the others coming up the stairwell and making their way to their bedchambers. I half expected Cade to stop, and at one point I was quite certain I felt his presence just beyond the wall, but soon his footsteps faded down the hall and were followed by the sound of a closing door.

I must have drifted to sleep then, because I was jerked awake some time later by the sound of a woman weeping. A wailing keen, not unlike the mournful wind I had heard last night, wafted through the walls of my darkened room, and I remembered Mrs. Hartley's strange expression when I had mentioned last night's storm. Had this been what my exhausted mind heard and confused with the wind?

I sat up in bed, shivering with fear as the muffled weeping continued. The thought of Desdemona, locked away in a coffin downstairs, sprang to my mind. I drove the thought away as quickly as it came. I would have to be insane to think that Desdemona, who had been dead nearly a week, could possibly be crying in the hallway. No, it had to be Eleanor or Lorraine, or even one of the maids.

The weeping grew closer, and I battled the urge to sink back against the mattress and cover my head. If someone in this house was in such pain, it was my duty as my father's daughter to offer them what comfort I could. I grabbed my Bible from the bedside table where it rested and slid from my bed. The ground was cold beneath my bare feet, but I hardly noticed as the weeping woman stopped outside my door. She moaned softly and a chill of apprehension rushed up my spine before I gathered my wits once more and hurried forward.

I eased the door open, peering up and down the eerily silent hall.

"Eleanor?' I called quietly. "Lorraine?"

A movement at one end of the hall caught my eyes, and I caught a glimpse of luminescent white fabric around the corner. I rushed to the end of the hallway, but found neither a turn to an adjoining corridor nor a door to another room.

The wall that blocked my pursuit was almost completely covered by a life-size portrait of my sister with Cade and Tabitha. In the portrait, they all looked stunning, even Tabitha, who had been painted as a normal child of three or four years old. Gone were the flat features, muted eyes and tiny teeth of the child I had met in the nursery. In her place was what I guessed to be my sister's version of the perfect child: angelic face, bouncing dark curls, and bright, intelligent eyes the exact color of our own. In truth, she looked just like I recalled Desi and myself looking at her age.

Both Tabitha and her mother were dressed in white gowns, the same bright white as the gown I'd seen from my doorway. Had I somehow caught a glimpse of this portrait from my bedroom door? I reached a shaking hand toward the portrait. Would Desdemona's dress feel as real as it looked?

A hand closed on my shoulder, and I turned, the breath draining from me in a dizzying wave of fear. My knees buckled and the Bible slipped from my numb fingers to the floor with a thud.

I heard a quiet curse as the hand released my shoulder and an arm encircled my waist to keep me upright.

I got my bearings quickly, recognizing the voice and arm through my fear. "Cade, you scared the life out of me."

"I spoke your name. I thought you heard me."

My hands were still shaking slightly, and I clutched them together to still them as I moved out of his grasp.

"What are you doing out here?" He shot one look toward the picture I'd been staring at, then moved so that he stood with his back to it, facing me. I wondered if the sight of Desi looking so alive was too much for him to bear. Was it guilt or grief that caused such a reaction? He repeated his question, his voice sharp with impatience.

"I heard someone crying. I came out to see if I could help them."

"Crying?" He looked genuinely confused.

I glanced down the hall to the open door separated from my own by two closed ones. There was no way he wouldn't have heard the crying woman.

"Don't tell me you didn't hear it. You had to have."

He shook his head. "I'm sorry, Fee, but I didn't hear anything except you. Perhaps you dreamed it."

Could I have been dreaming? It had been a stressful day, and I had been quite upset when I went to sleep. Could that have played a part in conjuring up such a vivid dream? Could my own grief for my sister haunt my dreams with wailing cries of distress? There was no other credible explanation, so I attempted to smile at my own foolishness.

"Perhaps you're right and it was nothing but a very realistic dream."

He touched my cheek. "You've had a hard time of it. Regardless of what the people here thought of Desdemona, she was your sister. Losing her has been difficult for you. Perhaps it would be a good idea for us to have the doctor stop in. He could prescribe something to help you sleep."

I shook my head. "No, I don't need medication. I'll be fine. It's just so difficult for me to believe Desi is dead. I thought she and I would have time to reunite. She died without ever knowing that I forgave her or wanted her forgiveness."

"What could you possibly have done that required her forgiveness?" he asked, his finger trailing gently down my cheek.

"It doesn't matter now," I murmured. My eyes closed as I enjoyed the sensation of his roughened skin against my face.

"Fee." Somehow he made my name sound like some precious word of adoration, and I wanted nothing more than to give in to the lure of it. I felt his gaze on me, and I opened my eyes. Instead of him, however, the picture behind him was what I saw.

I could almost believe the woman was me, but I knew better, as would anyone who knew us both. Although she had obviously ordered the artist to paint Tabitha without her flaws, Desi hadn't thought to have him cover her own. She was as she had always been, a beautiful woman, held apart from those who would love her by some unseen war she fought within herself. Her eyes, at once laughing and sorrowful, bored into mine, and I wished with all my heart I had known how to help her find her way.

Cade whispered my name again, and I forced my eyes from the portrait to his face. The sadness and longing I saw there filled me with fear and I backed away.

"Good night," I said, scooped my Bible from the floor, and hurried to my room.

Chapter Six

As the funeral procession wound its way up the incline behind the village church the next afternoon, I surveyed the sweeping view of the bay. Beyond the cemetery, on a short peninsula of land separated from the shore and Almenara by a rock jetty, the battered lighthouse stood sentinel. A balustrade encircled the uppermost parapet, and I imagined Desdemona there, so high above the seemingly endless expanse of water. I could well imagine how she had loved it there, with the sky stretched out around her as if she were a bird in flight. My mind took me to the dark thoughts I had refused to consider until then, and I imagined my sister, dark hair blowing in the wind as she balanced on the railing, arms outstretched beside her. A horrified cry escaped me as she leapt forward, her feet leaving solid ground and her body hurtling forward.

"Ophelia!" Cade gave me a quick shake, as if trying to awaken me from a nightmare.

Dazed by the vividness of what I'd imagined, it took me a moment to register the concern on his face and the shock on the faces of the people standing around us.

"What in God's name is wrong with you? You look as if you've seen a ghost."

The words reverberated through my mind, and I shook my head in denial. My father had prided himself

49

on his skepticism of all things supernatural and had sought to instill that same sensible disbelief in his daughters. He had his faith, of course, but was of a firm mind that ghosts and other such beings were nothing more than figments of overly fertile imaginations. I had questioned this principle more in the past twenty-four hours than ever in my life.

Cade placed an arm around my waist and guided me to the grave without another word, although he cast several worried glances in my direction. I stumbled along beside him, fighting to keep my eyes averted from the lighthouse and the shore below.

"Poor dear," Mrs. Hartley observed kindly, "grief has whipped her mind into a frenzy."

"Aye," a gentleman answered. "It's a shame what grief can do to a person."

"Grief, bah. I don't think it's grief has addled her brain at all." I recognized the sarcastic voice as that of Susan, the maid who'd witnessed that misbegotten kiss between Cade and me.

Cade's arm tightened on my waist, silent acknowledgment that he'd heard the speculations as well. Mrs. Hartley's hiss of disapproval assured me that the woman's sly innuendo would be dealt with upon our return home.

I faced forward, willing one foot in front of the other. I had never wanted to do anything less than I wanted to face what lay ahead. I didn't want to face the reality of my sister's death or my own inability to break through the betrayal and heartache that had kept us apart for the last years of her life.

No matter my reluctance to face it, however, we were soon there at the yawning hole that would be

Desdemona's final resting place, and with a nod from Cade, the funeral began.

The village pastor, a short bald man by the name of James Arnold, began to read from the Twenty-Third Psalm, and I let the dear familiar words wash over me.

"Thou preparest a table before me in the presence of mine enemies," Pastor Arnold read, and the words seemed to open up a dark cellar of questions inside me.

If Desdemona had indeed been murdered, someone had killed her. In all probability, someone here in this circle of village folk, servants, and family was Desdemona's mortal enemy.

I scanned each face, wishing I knew them well enough to suspect or discount them, whichever they warranted. But I knew none of them save a handful of servants and the family members who lived at Almenara. Each member of the Scott family seemed to hate Desdemona with equal measure, and if I were ever to gain answers about her death, I needed to know why.

A guttural cry jerked me from my reverie, and I watched in shocked fascination as a man rushed toward us. His clothes were tattered and torn, his dark blond hair long and unkempt. Around his shoulders he wore a cloak of the darkest navy silk, trimmed in what appeared to be dirty, matted ermine.

Cade's arm shot out, pushing me behind him as the man stopped between us and the open grave.

"Murderers!" Dark blue eyes swept wildly between us, encompassing the whole group. "All of you are murderers!"

"Devlin," Eleanor said from behind me, "darling, you must calm down."

She pushed her way between us and came to him,

her thick arm going around his shoulder and drawing him to her side.

"Calm down?" he snarled, shrugging her away but coming no closer to our group of mourners. "How can I be calm when my little bird, my Desdemona, is dead?"

He fell to his knees, his hands tearing at his hair as he sobbed out Desdemona's name.

I remembered then where I had heard his name. According to Mrs. Hartley, he was the artist who had painted the picture in Desi's morning room. Only a man of extreme talent could have captured the wild beauty of the place through Desdemona's eyes, making a simple picture seem like a glimpse into her soul. As was so often the case, it appeared that Devlin's extreme talent went hand in hand with madness. I was more than a little frightened when he looked up at me with those burning eyes and whispered my name.

"Ophelia," he said, pushing himself to his feet. He came forward, his hands outstretched. "She told me so much about you."

She had told him about me? Desi had told no one else of my existence, had obviously never even intended for them to learn she had a sister, much less a twin. Yet she had told this man. I was stunned into silence as he took my hand, his long, soft fingers circling mine.

He peered closely at me, his eyes mad with grief and something else I could not define, although I felt certain it was as close to real insanity as I had ever come.

"You aren't like her at all," he announced, dropping my hand. "She told me, of course, told me you and she were only alike in appearance, but I didn't

52

understand. Now I do. You do not have the war in you."

"The war?" I managed to croak through my fear.

"Darkness and light."

"Enough," Cade snapped, before Devlin could say more. "What the devil are you doing here, Devlin?"

Devlin turned toward Cade, his face turning cold with contempt. "I'm watching Desi's final scene, my friend. The sum of your soul-killing remorse."

He threw back the cloak with a grand flourish, and I heard Lorraine's sharp indrawn breath as a speck of silver flashed in the light.

"That is my cloak!" she squealed. "How on earth did you come to have it?"

His hands grasped possessively at the edges of the rich material, pulling it around him once more, and his eyes dared her to demand its return. When she remained silent, he smiled, and my breath caught in my throat. It was a somewhat evil smile, but it transformed his dirty, unshaven face into a thing of pure beauty. I knew with certainty why my sister would have been tempted by him.

"My little bird," he said, turning again to look at Desi's coffin, tears brimming in his eyes as his hand touched the smooth wooden exterior. "She snatched and pecked, took what wasn't hers and used it as her own. At least it was only a cloak she took from you."

With those words, he threw back his head and cawed, the sound echoing eerily across the cemetery and out over the water. Then, with the cloak flying out around him like broken wings, he dashed back into the forest from which he'd come.

"Proceed, please," Cade bid the pastor in an unemotional monotone, and Reverend Arnold picked up where he'd left off.

My mind raced, making it nearly impossible for me to concentrate on what was said during the remainder of the service. Had Devlin known that our father always called Desi and me his little birds? Had he been so close to my sister that she would have shared those details with him? Had his feelings for her been mutual? Had he been Desi's lover? Had he killed her?

A large black man I had seen working in the stables at Almenara began to sing in a low, pleasing baritone. It was a song I had chosen because Desi loved it when we were girls. As we grew, Desi changed and her love for hymns or anything related to my father's profession cooled. Still, I preferred to believe she had adhered to our faith internally, even if she rebelled against it outwardly.

I glanced over at Cade's grim face. Had Desi really loved him, or had it been her need to claim what was mine that drove her to him? He was staring intently at her coffin, brow furrowed and lips pursed. It was as much emotion as I had seen him portray over her death, and I found a strange sense of relief to see this small portrayal of grief.

He lifted his gaze to mine, and my breath caught in my throat. It wasn't grief that simmered in the dark depths of his gaze. It was anger.

Chapter Seven

Supper was waiting when we returned from the funeral, and Reverend Arnold and his very pregnant wife joined us at the table. Dennis Ames and Dr. Richard Scarborough also joined us, and I was quite relieved to have them all there. I felt certain there would be little likelihood of a recurrence of last night's drama, with guests in attendance.

We gathered at the table, Cade at one end, Calvin at the other, and the rest of us between them. Dennis sat at my left side and Dr. Scarborough on my right, and I was somewhat grateful to be sandwiched between the two of them rather than any of the Scott family. Perhaps if I endeavored to spend the meal talking quietly to my dinner companions, the others at the table would ignore me completely.

Between Cade and Dennis was an empty chair, and I tried to imagine what the last meal Desdemona had at this table had been like. Had it been closer to what I experienced last night, or the tense, solemn affair we were now enduring?

As silence lingered, the doctor leaned toward me to inquire about my wellbeing. He was a handsome man, with dark chestnut hair and eyes the color of warm brandy. I was aware he had been nearby when I envisioned the girl leaping from the lighthouse, and I wondered if he thought I might be as mad as Devlin appeared to be.

"I am a bit shocked by Desi's death and, of course, the nature of it, but I expect I will be fine, Doctor." I offered him my most confident smile, although I'm sure it looked more than a bit forced.

"Please call me Richard," he bid me, and I felt my smile ease into more relaxed lines. "And I, too, was shocked by your sister's murder. No one deserves to die in such a way, least of all Desdemona."

I was so overjoyed to hear someone express remorse over Desi's death that I nearly hugged him.

"Thank you," I said vehemently. "And you must call me Fee, as everyone else does."

"But your name is Ophelia, correct?"

"Yes."

"Then I think I would prefer to call you Ophelia. I have liked the name since my very first taste of Shakespeare, and it seems to fit you quite well."

I felt a blush steal up my cheeks as he spoke, and I inclined my head slightly in agreement.

"According to Desi, your mother was quite an admirer of Shakespeare," Dennis said, and I turned to include him in the conversation.

"My father always told us her love for Shakespeare was matched by her love of the theater."

"Miss Garrett, your father was a preacher, was he not?" Nellie Arnold queried brightly. She was dressed in a billowing dark blue dress, with a large ruffle around the neck and a significant number of smaller ones around the skirt. I wondered if it was the dress or her effervescent personality that seemed to overshadow the plain little man who was her husband.

"Yes, he was the pastor of a small country church.

He died five years ago."

"I'm terribly sorry. And your mother? Is she gone too?"

"My mother died giving birth to us. My father never quite got over the loss, but he continued on as well as he could and raised us alone."

I once again wondered if the loss of our mother, accompanied by my father's sad reservation and natural frugality, had intensified Desi's reckless need for affection. Even as a small child I threw myself into studying at his side, taking part in his extended reveries with my own silence and introspection, while she ran wild outdoors and in. As I grew older, I joined him in his work, becoming his hostess and helper as he performed the duties of his calling, and Desi found things outside of our world to occupy her time. Over the years, he and I forged a friendly bond that he and Desi never had. He loved her, and she loved him, but they had a basic inability to connect with each other in any more than the most simple, mundane ways that parents and children do.

"You have never married?"

I was a bit taken aback by the blunt question, but I gave a halfhearted chuckle and shook my head. I had the feeling that Nellie's inquisitiveness was natural and friendly as opposed to the calculated curiosity I had been subjected to by Lorraine since my arrival. "No. I tended to my father during a rather lengthy illness, and after he was gone, it just seemed I had somehow missed the boat."

"You're not that old at all, and there is always hope," she assured me, patting her husband's hand and smiling fondly at him. "Look at James and me. I was thirty-two when we met three years ago, and had all but given up on the prospect of marriage, let alone love. But here I am, happily married and expecting my first child."

She ran her hand over the swell of her belly, a soft smile on her face.

"Mrs. Arnold!" Eleanor's scandalized gasp told me that Almenara wasn't quite as distant from society as it would appear.

"For goodness' sake, Eleanor," Lorraine drawled. "It isn't as if no one's noticed she's pregnant."

"But to speak of it!"

"I'm sorry if I have offended you, Miss Scott," Nellie said easily, her lightly freckled face turning bright red and her hand dropping away from her stomach. I couldn't help but notice that her husband's hand caught hers, squeezing it gently before letting it go. "I just want Miss Garrett, and you, of course, to know that there is still hope. Love isn't out of reach for either of you."

I could feel Cade's eyes on me, and I prayed he would look away before I was forced to look in his direction. I didn't wish for a replay of last night, including another set of questions concerning my decision to care for my ailing father and leave Desi behind with him.

"Ophelia was in love when I knew her," Cade said quietly, and my eyes flew to his face.

"Cade, don't," I beseeched him, but he ignored me completely.

"She fell in love when we were in New Orleans. I have never seen such a wondrous sight as Ophelia in love."

"What happened?" Eleanor again. Curse her.

"I don't know," Cade admitted quietly, his eyes dark and questioning. "By the time I realized it was over, Fee was gone, Desi and I were married, and I never heard the full story."

All eyes turned in my direction as they waited for me to tell them the rest of the story. When I realized they weren't going to be satisfied until I said something, I cleared my throat and told them the most abbreviated version I could come up with.

"He was supposed to wait for me, but something happened. The telegram I received only said he was gone but offered no explanation."

"Gone?" Nellie repeated in horror. "Oh, poor darling, how horrible. Did you never find out what happened to him?"

"It was a long time ago," I assured her, grateful for her obvious assumption my former lover had died. "I'm surprised my brother-in-law still remembers."

When I met Cade's dark gaze, he had the grace to look away.

****

After dinner, we retired to the parlor, a rather ornate and dark room, where I was once again reminded of how little the inhabitants of Almenara cared that my sister was dead.

As if this were a normal social function, Eleanor sat at the piano in the corner, Lorraine stood beside her, and the two of them serenaded us with several lighthearted songs.

When I had partaken of their gaiety as long as I could stomach, I rose from my seat and excused myself quietly.

Cade made a move toward me, but I shook my head and left the room alone. Wanting to feel the warmth of the sun on my skin, I let myself out by the door at the end of the hall. Roses of every hue grew along the paths leading away from the house, changing from lush, double-bloomed bushes growing close to the house to scrappy, single-limbed vines as I neared the dunes.

"Ophelia, wait," Richard called from behind me.

I wanted nothing less than company, but I turned toward him out of common courtesy and forced a smile. I was struck once more by how handsome he was as he hurried down the path toward me.

"Do you mind if I join you?" he asked, holding out his arm.

"Of course not," I lied, slipping my hand into the crook of his arm as we strolled toward the shore.

"I can't imagine how their lack of mourning must hurt you. I'm sorry you must deal with such callousness."

"Thank you for that, Richard. It does hurt me to know that Desi left behind no one who mourns her, but it confuses me, as well. My sister and I had our differences, but I don't understand their complete lack of regard for her passing."

"There have always been dynamics in play at Almenara that only the inhabitants understand. Desdemona simply added another layer of misery to an already unhappy household."

"Have you known the family long, then?"

"I came here fifteen years ago, fresh out of medical school. I cared for the elder Mr. Scott during the last few years of his life."

"So you were here when Desdemona arrived? You knew her?" Besides Dennis Ames, he seemed to be the only person with kind feelings toward her.

"I did, although I can't say I knew her well. Desdemona was quite vehement in her dislike of me. She avoided me at all costs."

"Why?" I gasped. I could hardly imagine Desdemona disliking such a handsome man, much less one so kind and well-bred.

"Children with Tabitha's affliction are prone to all number of ailments, so I was here frequently enough that I could see things I would not normally have seen, even as a physician. I suppose my disapproval for your sister's behavior was obvious and something she didn't care for."

"What behavior?" I asked, although I felt certain I already knew. After all, both Calvin and Devlin had alluded to a relationship with her. It seemed even in marriage my sister had been unable to find the satisfaction with life that would keep her from wandering.

"I can see on your face that you've heard of some of your sister's less desirable activities. I never considered those sorts of things any of my business, however, and it was something else entirely that occasioned my lectures."

I could well imagine the reaction Desi had to being lectured by anyone, especially a man such as Richard. She had never taken discipline well and was used to men falling over themselves to please her. To be lectured by an attractive, articulate gentleman must have left her fuming.

"I felt she was sometimes careless with Tabitha,

you see," Richard continued. "She insisted on taking her up on the roof and out to the lighthouse at all hours of the day and night. She claimed Tabitha loved it, and perhaps she did, but changes in humidity, temperature, or even altitude can contribute to illness in a child. And any illness Tabitha contracts could easily prove fatal."

I felt myself blanch as he continued.

"I often told her that the child's wellbeing was at stake, but she simply laughed at what she called my overabundance of caution and went along her way."

"Perhaps she didn't comprehend the dangers," I offered in her defense.

"That was what I told myself when I went to Cade about my concerns. I hoped he could help make her understand, persuade her to be more careful." He pulled absently at his cravat as he gazed out at the lighthouse. "I have wondered over the last few days if that was the wisest course of action, but hindsight has a way of making us doubt our choices. There is nothing I can do to change it or the outcome."

"The outcome?"

"They say Cade confronted her that very afternoon, and there was a terrible row between the two of them. The servants swear—"

He broke off midsentence as Cade appeared on the path ahead of us.

My heart picked up its pace, a mixture of fear and attraction making it flutter in my chest. Even now, mere hours after my sister was buried, I longed to touch him. Everything I had heard since my arrival at Almenara pointed to him as her killer, but as he walked toward us, his jaw clenched and his eyes a stormy sea of emotion, all I could think of was the feel of his lips on mine.

"I have just been speaking with Ophelia about Tabitha," Richard informed him in a clipped voice. "I felt under the circumstances it was appropriate for her to know the facts."

"Of course," Cade agreed. "She should be informed of anything pertaining to Tabitha."

"Are the others gone already?" I asked Cade as the silence thickened between the two of them.

"Reverend Arnold and Nellie left a few moments ago. Dennis and Calvin are in a closed-door meeting. My guess is they're discussing the particulars of the crime they're so convinced I committed."

"Well, then, I suppose I've overstayed my welcome, and I should head home as well." Richard brought my hand to his lips, the soft kiss lingering on my skin a bit longer than necessary. "Should you need anything, Ophelia, please call on me."

"Should she be in need of medical assistance, Richard, you can rest assured we will contact you right away," Cade assured him in a tight, cold voice. "I doubt she will need you for anything else."

"Of course." Richard smiled at me and, with a very impertinent wink, turned and strode up the walk to the house.

"He seems quite a nice man," I observed as Cade and I walked side by side toward the house.

"Richard is a good man," Cade agreed, "but I don't like you walking out alone with him."

"Good heavens, why not?"

"He's an unmarried man and you're an unmarried woman. You certainly have enough sense to realize it isn't appropriate."

I laughed, and he looked at me sharply.

63

"What's so funny?"

"I find it rather amusing that you should lecture me on acceptable behavior when your cousins just hosted an afternoon soiree, complete with lively, gay entertainment, on the day of my sister's funeral."

"I apologize for their behavior," he said, appearing to be properly chastised. "I had no idea they intended to sing such joyous, bawdy songs. But I warned you they didn't mourn her."

"Why do they dislike her so much?"

"If I had to pinpoint one reason, I'd say it was her ability to ruin everything she touched and then flit away from whatever it was, never to think of it again."

Although it was a rather cryptic answer that gave me no real details at all, I understood it. After all, it was exactly what she'd done to me.

"Did they dislike her enough to kill her?"

"No." I'm sure he hoped his curt tone would discourage further questioning, but I was not to be so easily swayed.

"Someone did."

"So it appears."

"And it wasn't you."

"How can you be so sure?" he growled, leaning closer to me.

"You don't scare me, Cade," I said, inhaling his fury and the rich masculine scent of him. "No matter how many people say you killed her or how many times you let them say it, I'm not scared of you."

"You should be." His voice was soft, injured, and he turned his face away so that he was staring at the lighthouse instead of me.

"Why?" I cried, grasping his face and forcing him

to look at me. "Why should I be frightened of you? And who should they look to if not you?"

"Look to everyone, Fee!" he exclaimed, his eyes wild with pain. "We all hated her with equal measure, and every single person at Almenara, and even some beyond these walls, had a reason to want her dead."

Had she really hurt so many people? I wanted to scoff in disbelief, to tell him he was wrong, but how could I? How could I say that Desdemona wouldn't hurt people she barely knew, when she'd broken my heart without remorse?

"Maybe one of them killed her. Calvin or Lorraine or Eleanor even. What about Devlin? He's obviously unhinged. Couldn't he have done it?"

He grasped me by the shoulders, hard and quick enough that a gasp escaped me. "Don't you understand, Ophelia? I have no idea where to look or who to point a finger at."

"So you're willing to take the blame and hang for her murder?"

"Desdemona was my wife. Mine. Regardless of what she'd done or how much I disliked her, she was mine to protect, and I failed."

"But you didn't kill her," I insisted.

"Neither you nor I will ever convince anyone otherwise."

"So you won't fight the charges?"

"I'll plead not guilty. I'll give them my testimony," he said. "That's all I can do. The rest will be up to the judge and jury."

Taking my hands in his, he smiled sadly.

"I don't want to hang, Fee, but I'm fairly certain I will."

Before I could reply, Calvin called out to him from the doorway. We were silent as we walked back to the house, and I wondered desolately if what he said was true. Would he hang in spite of his innocence?

Chapter Eight

That night, despite the jumble of questions and emotions inside me, I fell into an exhausted slumber as soon as my head hit the pillow. I awoke the next morning feeling as tired as I would have had I not slept at all, with only a vague recollection of the nightmares that had plagued my sleep. The sound of weeping and a woman's screams still echoed in my head as I made my way down to breakfast. Outside the house, thunder rumbled, and I could hear a steady torrent of rain beating at the roof and windows. Perhaps this time the wailing screams had really only been the wind and rain blowing against the windows.

As I dressed, I silently planned the day ahead of me. Except for a few moments here and there, Cade and I had not had much chance to discuss the particulars of Desi's death or the reasons he was thought to have murdered her. I assumed he would be with his attorney for most of the day, even though I had heard no mention of an attorney or the date of the trial on the horizon. I wanted to know the evidence they had against him. Was his arrest based solely on what the servants said? Or was there more? I couldn't fathom him as a murderer, but I had no idea what motives anyone else might have had. I would spend my day asking questions and finding answers regarding my sister's life at Almenara, as well as her death.

Regardless of our differences, I owed her that.

Determined to gain at least some of the answers I sought before nightfall, I marched into the dining room with my head held high.

Lorraine and Calvin were already at the table, and I bid them good morning as I went to the sideboard to retrieve a cup of coffee and a puffed pastry filled with strawberries and cream. The smell of bacon caught my attention, and I placed a few strips on my plate. It would be a busy day, and I needed strength and stamina to carry out my mission.

The couple inquired how I slept as I settled into a chair, and after several minutes of small talk, we were joined by Eleanor and Cade.

"I received word that the judge will be here a week from Monday. We'll pick a jury and try your case then," Calvin informed him as Cade took a seat.

I felt the blood drain from my face. Monday was four days away, meaning Cade's trial would begin in less than two weeks. There was barely enough time for Cade to retain a lawyer, if he hadn't already done so, much less prepare a defense.

Cade's face remained impassive, and had it not been for the slight tick in his jaw, I would have wondered if he'd even heard.

"Will your attorney be coming to Almenara?" I asked him.

"No."

"So you are free to go to him?"

"There won't be a lawyer, Fee. It won't do me a bit of good, as there's little hope of anyone believing I'm innocent, with or without an attorney. I'll speak for myself."

"Cade, you can't. It's a murder trial. You could hang." A hint of hysteria edged my voice, and I grasped his hand. "What about Tabitha?"

Pain clouded his eyes as he looked down at me.

"I hoped you would take care of her when I'm gone."

"That is out of the question," Lorraine protested. "Calvin and I will care for her."

I had not seen any prior sign that Lorraine cared about my niece or her wellbeing. Although I had been here only two days, I had not heard Tabitha's name cross her brightly painted lips. Yet she looked positively panicked by the thought of me caring for the child.

"Why?" The word escaped me before I could stop it, and although I knew it was a rude, inexcusable question, I let it hang there in the air between us.

Lorraine sputtered, shot a look toward Calvin, and gathered a regal attitude about her. "Because we love her, of course, and we can offer her a more stable home than a nearly impoverished spinster aunt."

"She will need special care her entire life," I said, ignoring her disparaging characterization of my circumstances. "Are you willing to give her that?"

"Of course," Calvin answered smoothly. "We will ensure she receives the best of care."

I wondered where he intended her to receive that care. I sincerely doubted their intention was to keep her here at Almenara. As soon as the ink was dry on the guardianship papers, they would ship her off to live in an institution. Of that, I was certain.

Beneath my hand, Cade's palm turned up and his fingers wrapped around mine.

"I will give it some thought," Cade assured them, "and I will make arrangements by the time the trial starts."

Lorraine looked as if she wanted to protest, but she clamped her mouth shut when Calvin shook his head.

"Of course, you must consider all options, Cade," Eleanor agreed. "We would expect no less. After all, Tabitha is the very reason we find ourselves in this predicament."

I looked at her sharply, and she shrugged. "I assumed Dr. Scarborough had already told you about the argument Cade and Desi had."

"No," I said, partly because I didn't want to betray Richard's trust and partly because I hoped she would enlighten me as he had been about to do.

Ignoring Cade's glare and Calvin and Lorraine's amusement, Eleanor leaned toward me, her dark eyes sparkling with excitement.

"What did you think of Devlin? Isn't he beautiful?"

"Stark raving mad is more like it," her sister-in-law snapped, going along with the abrupt change in conversation. "Calvin intends to search for him as soon as this rain lets up. Once found, he'll be transported to the nearest asylum."

"He is not mad!" Eleanor protested shrilly.

"Do you really think he will love you now that Desdemona is dead, Eleanor?" Lorraine drawled. "Do you think he will forget she existed or that she was his lover? Do you really think he'll turn to you?"

"Yes!" Eleanor screeched as she leapt from the table. "Yes, that is what I think. He loved me first, and would love me still if she hadn't stolen him away."

"He never loved you, Eleanor," Calvin said quietly.

"Now, sit down and finish your meal."

"He loved me," she insisted as she settled back into her seat. She looked from her brother to Cade. "Don't you remember when he visited Almenara during your school recesses? He always noticed me then, didn't he, Cade?"

Cade paused as he lifted his fork to his mouth, and offered her a gentle, indulgent smile. "Of course I remember. Your mother remarked on the hope she had for your future each time she saw the two of you together."

"Thank you," she breathed, and I thought she might burst into tears she appeared so grateful for his agreement.

"Why must you encourage her delusions, Cade?" Lorraine asked him.

"What I said is true. She and Devlin were inseparable when he visited us in our school days. They had much in common, and her mother did look upon them with hope for Eleanor's future."

"What happened then?"

"Devlin went mad," Calvin answered dryly, successfully bringing their conversation back full circle and causing his sister to let lose a howl of outrage before marching from the room.

Chapter Nine

I stood in the nursery door an hour later, watching Cade as he knelt beside the chair where his daughter sat. Reciting a poem about a spider, he walked his fingers up her arm, wiggling them just beneath her chin. Each repetition brought about a smile and a laugh from Tabitha, accompanied by a low chuckle from Cade himself.

Unaware of my presence, Cade let her touch his face, her small stubby hands exploring his features. He named each one as she touched it, and when she came to his mouth, he puckered his lips and kissed her hands with loud smacking sounds.

Tears sprang to my eyes, and I turned away. Had Desi cared so little for the two of them that she had been unfaithful to Cade and endangered Tabby's life? Had they belonged to me, I would have treasured them both, and loved them with every fiber of my being. Nothing short of death would have separated me from either of them.

Of course, they weren't mine. Desi had made sure of that. Like my most well-loved doll, my favorite book, and the blue velvet hair ribbons Mrs. Dupree gave me for my thirteenth birthday, Desdemona had claimed Cade as her own simply because she could. I remembered Devlin's words at the funeral, when he described her as a little bird that snatched and pecked, took what wasn't hers and used it as her own. I had always found the things she had taken from me after she was done with them, used and faded, cast aside as if she had never really cared for them at all.

"Fee?" Eleanor called out as I passed her room. She sat on the bed, dressed in a brilliant blue riding habit, pulling boots on her feet. "Would you care to go for a ride this morning? Lorraine usually rides with me, but she has a headache this morning, and I hate to go alone."

I didn't ride often, but Mrs. Dupree had allowed Desi and me free use of her stable, and I was a capable equestrienne. A ride through the countryside seemed a good time to learn what I could about Desi's death from Eleanor.

"I would love to go, but I haven't brought a riding habit."

"Your sister had several. Perhaps you could use one of them."

"Yes, of course. Should I ask Cade first?"

"Heavens, no. I'm sure Cade won't mind." She placed a hand through my arm and accompanied me to my room. Dory was there, straightening the counterpane on the newly made bed.

"Dory, fetch Miss Garrett one of her sister's riding habits."

"Yes, miss," she said with a small curtsy.

"A black one," I added. "Something suitable for mourning."

"Do you really intend to wear mourning clothes for six months?" Eleanor asked as she wandered around the room, her hand gliding over the bed, the chairs by the window, and each item on the dressing table.

"Yes," I said, although I doubted it was true. No one at home would think less of me for wearing anything other than black and here, it was obvious, no one cared one way or the other. My sister had only been buried yesterday, however, and I would not quit wearing it today.

"Lorraine was right, you know, when she said Desdemona wouldn't have worn black for you."

"That makes no difference. It's the right thing to do."

"Yes, I suppose you're right." She cocked her head. "Don't you find it odd that the two of you are so different?"

Dory entered the room with a black riding habit and a jaunty black hat with a small veil and a gray plume on the side.

"I'll meet you at the stable," Eleanor said. "I'll have the horses readied while you dress."

The sun had been shining earlier in the day, but when I came outside it had moved behind the clouds, and the air felt cool with coming rain.

"It may not be a very long ride," Eleanor said as the groom led the horses to us, "but we'll be home before the rain, I'm sure."

She took the reins of a pretty chestnut mare, and the groom handed me those of the dappled gray that trailed behind her.

"Desdemona called her Dove," Eleanor told me, "And this is my Angel."

As the groom helped me mount, I swallowed my tears. My father had always compared Desi and me to the birds that frequented the countryside around our home. He told us Desi was a spirited, high-flying barn swallow, while I was a calm, down-to-earth mourning dove. Had she remembered me when she'd christened the pretty gray horse?

We rode away from the house, heading down the drive in companionable silence. As we passed the gatehouse, Eleanor pointed toward a small well in front of it.

"When Cade and I were young, we were certain sea nymphs had a tunnel between the sea and that old well. I have no idea where the idea came from, probably our nurse, Miss Loy, who always had a superstitious tale to tell."

"Did she believe Almenara was haunted?"

"Of course. Ever since I can remember, the maids have recounted ghostly encounters in the hallways and empty rooms. It's the way it is in old houses. Desdemona wasn't the first wife to die under mysterious circumstances at Almenara."

In any house older than a few years, someone was bound to have died, so I wasn't really surprised by her declaration. I was shocked by her next words, however.

"Calvin's first wife leapt over the side of the lighthouse, you know." She glanced toward me, as if gauging my reaction. "He found her body on the rocks below."

"How sad," I murmured, remembering the woman I'd imagined balancing on the railing during Desi's funeral.

"Calvin found her. I'll never forget that day. He and Cade had been in a heated row, arguing as always, about Cade's control of the purse strings and Amelia's spending. She was a beautiful girl, spoiled by her parents and used to the very best of everything. She

75

married Calvin against her parents' wishes, and he was determined to prove to them he could care for her as well as they did."

I remained silent, waiting for her to continue.

"Our grandfather left Calvin and me well enough off that we could both be independent, but Almenara is our home. Luckily, he had the foresight to arrange things so that we were able to stay here if we so desired. After all, had our father not died, Calvin would have inherited Almenara instead of Cade."

This bit of information pricked my ears. Why had Mrs. Hartley not mentioned it when she told me of how they all came to live here? Was it common knowledge?

"Is that why they dislike each other so?" I asked.

"That is part of it, yes. When we came here with our mother, our father had been dead for several years. Our home was destroyed by Union troops soon after his death, and we lived by selling the few possessions my mother was able to salvage. She never wanted to come here, because of the way they treated her when she married our father. When it finally came down to starvation or groveling at the feet of our grandfather, she brought us here. We had lived without basic necessities, much less the luxuries of Almenara, for years. To arrive here and find Cade firmly ensconced as the heir apparent drove a wedge between him and Calvin that no amount of time can overcome." She looked at me. "You knew Cade when he was younger. Surely you can see the changes in him. He was always a kind man, warm and loving and ready to take care of anyone who needed his protection. Calvin was a good boy when we were children, but as the years have passed I think he has realized how much he lost to

Cade, and he's grown cruel and taunting. Cade has been determined to bury his guilt at having inherited Almenara and prove himself as a worthy master, while Calvin has seemed determined to be a thorn in his side."

"So they have always bickered as they do now?"

"Yes, but at times it has gone well past bickering to outright pugilism."

I had witnessed that on my first day at Almenara, when Calvin hinted at a relationship with Desi. Now, I wondered if what he said was true.

"Was your brother having an affair with my sister?"

Eleanor let out a tinkling laugh, and shook her head. "I don't think so, but Calvin did everything in his power to make Cade believe they were."

"What a horrible thing to do!" I exclaimed.

Eleanor shrugged. "It is how the two of them have always been."

We had ridden to the edge of the meadow, where the land became a promontory that overlooked the shore and ocean below.

To our left, I could see the lighthouse, and I shivered as a cloud passed over it. Was it merely a coincidence that both Cade and Calvin had lost their wives there?

A large black horse stood just outside the door, and as we watched, a cloaked figure came out of the lighthouse and mounted the horse. I would have known him anywhere, even without the way my breath caught in my throat as he thundered down the shore, past the spot where we stood and off into the distance, as if the demons of hell were on his heels.

"If anything is haunted at Almenara, it's the people," Eleanor said, as a crash of thunder shook the earth beneath our feet. "And Cade is the most haunted of all."

Chapter Ten

Our ride home was silent, as we gave the horses their heads and let them gallop back to the safety of the stables. We beat the rain by mere seconds, and dashed across the courtyard and into the house.

"Good Lord!"

I looked toward the spot where Richard Scarborough stood, bag in hand, beside the stairs. His face was white with shock and, for a moment, I feared he might keel right over.

"Richard, are you ill?" I hurried toward him, but with a slight shake of his head, he seemed to get hold of himself.

"I'm fine. It was just a momentary shock to see you come through the door, looking just like Desdemona."

"Oh, I'm so sorry," I said with an apologetic smile. "I didn't even think about that."

I pulled my hat from my head, and a few plump curls fell loose around my shoulders. He swallowed hard, his color returning with a vengeance as his gaze wandered over my face and form. For the first time in many years, I felt the power an attractive woman wields over a virile man.

I could not ignore the desire that lit his face, but I had no idea what to do with it. So I did what I had always done in situations where I was uncertain of my next move. I excused myself and rushed up the stairs to my room.

Once I had washed up and changed, I emerged, hopeful that Richard was gone and Cade had returned.

As I wandered through the downstairs rooms, I passed the ballroom where Desi's coffin had been. The black velvet had been removed from the mirrors, and Mrs. Hartley was instructing two young maids on washing their gleaming surfaces. Both of the girls looked scared out of their wits, and I wondered if they were more frightened of Mrs. Hartley's disapproval or of the ghosts rumored to haunt this room.

"Miss Garrett." Mrs. Hartley greeted me with a smile and followed me into the hallway. "How can I help you?"

"I'm looking for Cade. Do you happen to know where I can find him?"

"He's not here, miss. He left shortly after breakfast, saying he'd be home after dark."

"Eleanor and I saw him on the shore when we were riding. Would he still be out in this weather?"

"He's always been one to love this sort of weather. He used to lecture Mrs. Scott about going up to the lighthouse in the rain, but he'd be galloping about on that big black horse of his in the very same storm."

My suddenly fertile imagination conjured up a picture of Cade, wet shirt plastered to his chest, as his stallion's gait ate up the sand along the coastline. When had I given up my usually studious and peaceful mind to such imaginings? And when had I ever felt the way I felt right now, as the thought of him taking me up beside him on the beast's back made me weak in the knees?

"I believe he was going to see his solicitor. He was

dressed for business when he left. He asked that the carriage be ready when he returned from his ride."

"Perhaps he's decided to hire someone to handle his defense," I said hopefully.

Mrs. Hartley's hand went to her chest, and tears filled her eyes. "Poor boy, to think he only has a few more days on—"

I stopped her before she could speak the words that would remind me of the dire possibility of Cade's death.

"Perhaps the matter is not so decided as everyone thinks," I offered.

"Oh, miss, I would like to believe that. But we all heard him threaten to kill her."

"Yes, someone mentioned that to me. They were in the midst of an argument, I believe."

"They were in a terrible row, and I think he only spoke it in anger. But only a few days later, she was dead."

"What were they arguing about?"

"That I don't know, Miss Garrett." She seemed to gather herself, and offered me a small smile. "Besides, I've already said too much. It's something you'd best discuss with Mr. Cade."

I knew she was right, and I said so, but as I turned to go, she grasped my arm.

"Will you be taking Tabitha with you when you leave, miss?"

"I sincerely hope Tabitha will remain here with her father."

"Of course, but I hate to think of what would happen to her here if Mr. Cade were gone. She'll be the only one in the way of them then."

"Do you believe someone in the household would harm her?" I exclaimed. "Who?"

"They've never done a thing to make me think it, Miss Garrett. Never uttered an unkind word about the poor little thing, but should Mr. Cade die, she will inherit it all. And their hatred of him will turn on her."

"Were you here when Calvin's first wife died?"

"I've been here for thirty-four years, miss. I was here when Miss Amelia became Mr. Calvin's wife, and I was here when she died."

"Was there ever any question about her death? I mean, were they certain it was a suicide?"

"I wasn't privy to the investigation, Miss Garrett."

"But doesn't it seem strange that she and Desdemona would die in the same way?"

"It is nothing but a sad coincidence, and there was nothing to be gained by accusing anyone of her murder."

"Was Calvin the sheriff then?" I hammered at her, although I could tell by the way her eyes darted toward the shadowed recesses of the hallway, her hands working the white lace of her collar, she was fearful of overstepping her bounds.

"No, miss. Mr. Calvin was only a young man, and there was another sheriff then. From what I remember of that time, he declared it a suicide and said he found no evidence to charge Mr. Cade or anyone else with her death."

"Cade?" I cried. "Why on earth would he have charged Cade with her murder?"

Mrs. Hartley's fingers stilled, and her serious blue eyes met mine. "Cade was with her at the lighthouse when she died."

Nothing could have shocked me more, and I reached out to steady myself against the wall.

"Ophelia?" Richard's low, rich voice was actually a welcome sound as he rounded the corner behind us. With a few quick strides, he was beside me, his arm around my waist as he led me to a chair.

"I'm fine," I croaked. When he ignored my words and placed fingers on my wrist to feel my pulse, I jerked away from him. "Really, Richard, I'm quite fine."

"Very well, then." He offered me his hand and helped me to my feet. As he placed my hand in the crook of his arm, Mrs. Hartley excused herself and went back into the ballroom.

Richard guided me to Desdemona's morning room and closed the door firmly behind us. It was quite improper for us to be behind closed doors alone, but I didn't care. I needed to talk things over with someone, and Richard seemed willing to listen.

"Do you care to tell me what shocked you so badly?" he asked, taking a seat in the chair across from mine.

I told him what I had learned of Calvin's late wife. When I was done, he sat back in his seat.

"Oh, yes, poor Amelia. That girl was a spoiled, naïve little princess with just enough beauty to blind a man to her faults. She was Devlin's sister, you know."

"Devlin's sister?" Why had Eleanor not thought it important to mention that to me? Did anyone here ever tell the entire story, or did they always leave out some pertinent bit of information?

"It seems some mental instability is in their blood. It leads Devlin to live as a hermit in the woods, alone and demented, and led Amelia to dash herself upon the rocks below the lighthouse."

"And Cade was with her when she did it?"

"To be fair, Cade was devastated by her death."

"But that is why he isn't fighting his accusations this time, isn't it? That's why he feels it useless to proclaim his innocence?"

"It will be hard to find anyone who doesn't remember Amelia or didn't think of her death as soon as they learned of Desdemona's. The similarities in the way they died will make it nearly impossible for him to get a fair trial."

"I must find a way to prove his innocence!" I cried, leaping to my feet. I turned toward him. "We can't possibly let him hang."

"Of course, we can't," he murmured, but his eyes were on the picture above the mantel.

"Mrs. Hartley says Devlin painted it," I said. "It is very realistic, isn't it?"

"Was she always so enamored of birds?"

"Oh, yes, always. I think, if she could have, she would have flown through the air with them. Whenever we wanted to find her, back home, we had only to look in the highest branches of the tallest tree."

"If one wanted to find her here, one had only to traipse out to the lighthouse. She was easy prey for whoever wanted her dead."

"I know the Scotts disliked her immensely, Richard, but there is a huge difference in disliking someone and killing them."

"There's a fine line between love and hate."

"So you believe Cade killed her?" My voice sounded much angrier than I meant for it to, and his eyebrows rose a little at my tone.

"No, not at all. Cade wasn't by any means the only man in love with your sister."

"So I've heard. Were you one of them?"

"Only a little." He chuckled. "And only for a moment. Truthfully, Ophelia, there wasn't much I even liked about her once I got to know her."

"She must have hated that," I observed.

He shrugged. "I don't think it bothered her in the least. I've told you, she disliked me quite vehemently."

The reminder that Desi had ignored his advice concerning Tabitha brought me to my next question.

"Do you believe any of the Scotts would harm Tabitha if Cade weren't here?"

His answer was quick and put me more at ease. "Why would they? If they are her guardians, then Calvin would have full control over everything. It isn't likely Tabby will ever marry or have children of her own. Most children like her succumb to their affliction long before marriageable age. If you are her guardian, Cade may leave you a stipend to care for her, but you would never control Almenara or the family's assets. With Cade out of the picture, they will simply put her away somewhere and go on as if she doesn't even exist."

"That is true, I suppose."

He stood from his seat and went to the window.

"It seems the rain has nearly stopped. I should leave before it picks up again."

I rose to show him to the door, and he took my hand in his. His touch was gentle but firm as he lifted it to his lips.

"You are quite different from your sister, Ophelia,

and I find the more I know you, the more I like you. I would like your permission to call on you during your stay at Almenara."

"Richard," I began, but he cut me off with a tender smile.

"Don't answer me now. We will see each other when I visit Tabitha. You will come to know me, and you can make your decision when you feel comfortable. I won't pressure you by asking again. I will simply await your decision."

I returned his smile. "I am flattered by your interest, Richard, and I look forward to your future visits."

We walked to the door, and I watched him hurry to his carriage. I returned his wave with a lift of my hand and turned away from the door.

Lorraine stood at the bottom of the staircase, watching me with an interested gleam in her eyes. Her mouth curved into a patronizing smile.

"Do I detect some interest between you and our good doctor?"

"He is a kind man, and I consider him a friend."

She smiled again and came toward me.

"Let me show you around the house, Ophelia. We share our niece, after all, and it would be good for us to get to know one another. We will be all she has once Cade is gone."

Although Mrs. Hartley had given me a brief overview of which rooms belonged to whom on the day of my arrival, I was happy to get a more in-depth tour and fell into step beside Lorraine.

"This hall is a mirror image of the other, for the most part," she said as we walked down the hall opposite the ballroom. "The billiard room replaced the ballroom on this one."

She opened a door to a room covered in a vast expanse of wood paneling, with dark leather-upholstered chairs, billiard and poker tables.

We followed the hall to Calvin's study, her morning room, and a small glass-paned conservatory at the end of the hall. The conservatory jutted out enough from the rest of the house that one could see the dunes and a small sliver of the lighthouse beyond the other corridor, which blocked most of the view. The rest of the conservatory faced a garden quite similar to the one I could see from my own room.

"They say this was my predecessor's favorite room," she said, as she ran her hand across the delicate white spinet. "Some of the maids fear her ghost abides here, just as Desdemona's walks the upstairs corridor."

"I thought Desi haunted the ballroom."

She rolled her eyes and laughed.

"The ballroom is a catch-all for everyone who has ever been carried out of Almenara feet first. Eventually, I suppose, I shall join them all in that dreadful room, frightening the next crop of maids by dancing the jig in the middle of the night."

I couldn't help but smile at the image her words conjured.

She sighed. "The thing I've always wondered is why, if Amelia was willing to throw herself from the lighthouse in order to escape life here, she would return to haunt the halls."

"Do you believe she killed herself?"

"Of course. What else would I believe?" When I didn't answer, she led me out of the room. "That Cade killed her? Is that what you heard?"

"I was led to believe he was a suspect."

"Yes, I suppose some might say that." She was silent for only a moment before asking, "Will you remain at Almenara until after Cade's trial?"

"Yes."

"Will you sit in on the trial, do you think?"

"I should think so."

"It will be difficult for you."

"I think I shall manage well enough."

She opened several doors, revealing guest rooms, before opening one to a bedroom that I immediately knew had belonged to my sister. The faint scent of her perfume still lingered there, and I wanted nothing more than to enter, to search for some small piece of the girl I remembered, in the belongings scattered about.

"Desdemona's room," she said. "Just the way she left it before he killed her."

"Do you really believe Cade capable of killing her?"

She gave me a sly glance. "I believe a man betrayed is capable of many things."

"What about a woman?" I shot back, thinking of Calvin's innuendo the day of my arrival.

She laughed outright and pushed the next door open. "This is Cade's room."

Dim light slipped through the crack in the drawn curtains, and the red embers in the hearth made the room warm and cozy. It was the massive bed in the center of the room that captured my attention, however, as another uncharacteristic spell of imagination came over me and I imagined Cade there, illuminated by the flickering light of the fireplace, a welcoming smile on his handsome face.

I stepped back with a startled gasp, and she pulled the door shut quickly. She didn't speak a word about my reaction to his room, and for that I was grateful. There was no way to explain without sounding like a lovelorn fool. But something about the smile that played about her mouth told me she guessed where my mind had taken me.

We came to the picture at the end of the hall, and Lorraine made a sound of disgust.

"Your sister had this picture painted last year, proof of her indiscretion and idiocy."

Perhaps I should have defended Desi instead of nodding my head in silent agreement. But there was something intrinsically wrong with having Tabitha painted to look so different than she was. Had it been the artist's eye or Desi's that caught the cold anger in Cade's eyes, the tightness of his jaw and the cruel twist of his smile? If I had seen Desi before her death, would she have looked at me with sad reproach as she did from the portrait, as if she blamed me for lack of the happiness she had sought and never found?

"Let's move on."

On the next corridor were the room she shared with her husband, Eleanor's room, and at the end, the nursery suite where Tabby spent her days and nights.

I peeked into the nursery, where Tabby was awake and eating a soft cookie as Janie put folded clothes into a short squat bureau. Upon seeing me, Tabby squealed and banged her hands on the table. I could do nothing less than enter the nursery and scoop her into my arms.

"You'll be a mess, miss," Janie warned. "She has a way of making the biggest mess with her cookies."

"I don't mind," I said, as the child touched my cheeks with hands covered in wet sticky crumbs. I giggled my delight, and Tabby joined in with a chortle of her own.

"There is one more thing I'd like to show you, Fee," Lorraine said from the doorway.

"Can Tabby come?" I asked, reluctant to put my niece down again.

The woman looked a bit put out but nodded her agreement. "Of course."

I followed her to the end of the hall, expecting to see a dead end like the one where the portrait hung in the other hall. Instead, there was a small door at the end of the hallway. On the other side of it, a narrow set of steps led up to the roof.

Although the worst of the storm had calmed momentarily, the sky remained gray and overcast, and a light, steady drizzle still hit the sides of the large copper cistern that caught water to be piped through the house. Lorraine stepped onto the roof and beckoned me forward.

"You can see the lighthouse from here," she said as I hung back just inside the door.

My sister's love of heights was in direct contrast to my fear of them, and I shook my head. "It's too damp. I don't want Tabitha to catch a chill."

Lorraine sighed heavily. "That's why she should have been left in the nursery."

"I had no idea you were going to show me the roof, Lorraine. Besides I didn't want to leave her in the nursery."

"It's the only place she's safe, Ophelia," she said. "You'd do well to remember that."

With that, she stepped inside, locked the door behind us, and led us back down the hall.

She continued on, while I stopped at the nursery. I desperately hoped that I had only imagined the ominous warning in Lorraine's words as I clung to Richard's sensible assurance that Tabby was in no danger from Calvin and Lorraine.

"Does Tabby go outside?" I asked Janie, trying to sound nonchalant.

"Sometimes, if it's very nice outside, we go for a stroll in the garden. She sickens easily if it's too damp or too cold out, so I'm careful to take her only on nearly perfect days." She hastily added, "I would never take her out on a day like today."

Realizing she felt I was questioning her ability to care for Tabby, I offered her a smile of encouragement.

"You take wonderful care of her, Janie. Please don't think I doubt that. Something Lorraine said just made me wonder if she was ever taken outside."

"Well, thank you, miss. I try to take good care of her. Poor little mite."

"Janie, it appears that Tabby may be returning home with me. If that happens, would you be willing to come to stay with us? I'm not sure of the salary yet, but there would be room and board included."

"Oh, I would love to come with you, miss. I've been looking after Tabby since she was a baby, and I would miss her terribly if she were to leave. I would have to discuss it with my parents, of course. I have to make sure they could do without me being so close at hand. But they know how much I love Tabby, and I can send them money when I have some."

"Will a move like that upset her, do you think?"

"I'm sure she'll miss her father. Mr. Cade is here every night to tuck her in, and he comes in nearly every morning and afternoon to spend a bit of time with her. If we take her familiar things with us, though, I'm sure she'd do fine after a while."

"What about the others? Do any of them come to visit her?"

"Others?" She stared at me blankly before understanding dawned on her. "Oh, you mean Mr. and Mrs. Scott and Miss Eleanor? No, not one of them comes to the nursery. When Dennis Ames stops in, he sometimes comes up to say hello, and Dr. Scarborough comes by on a regular basis. But none of the others. Even when I take her out for a stroll, they rarely even offer her a word or gesture."

I nodded. That was exactly what I had feared when Lorraine voiced her desire to keep Tabitha here with them. Even Richard had confirmed that she would be sent away, but at least, as he said, she would be safe.

****

Dinner was a quiet affair without Cade at the table. No one spoke much at all, except to make the most ordinary of observances. We had just been served the main course when Cade came through the front door, his coat and hat dripping as if he had walked home instead of ridden in the enclosed carriage Mrs. Hartley claimed he had taken into the city.

"Did you have trouble with the carriage, sir?" Mrs. Hartley asked as she took his soaked garments.

"No, the carriage is fine. I decided to brave the elements on Sampson's back tonight. I thought a good rain-lashing might straighten out my head." He divested himself of his sodden boots and traipsed up the stairs without even looking our way.

"He rode poor Sampson home at breakneck speed, no doubt," Lorraine surmised.

"He'll catch his death of cold, out in this weather," Eleanor fretted.

"Maybe he prefers that to hanging," Calvin said, and although he tried to sound cruel, I thought I detected a hint of worry creasing his brow. Did he realize his cousin didn't deserve to hang, and if he had doubts, why was he so insistent on seeing it through?

Chapter Eleven

The rain was still hammering against the windows when I awoke the next morning, and with a groan I got up and dressed. I had always been a sound sleeper and an early riser, but the fitful sleep I had endured since arriving at Almenara was taking a toll on my usual bright attitude toward morning. Waking up to continuing gray skies also hampered my ability to greet the morning with my customary enthusiasm.

I had hoped to go for another early morning ride, to explore the beach between Almenara and the lighthouse before speaking to Cade. The stormy weather and the chill that seemed to sink into the room changed my plans, however, and after dressing in a thick gray dress, I went in search of Cade.

I found him in his study, standing at the large window from which he could see the lighthouse. He spoke before I announced my presence, and I wondered if he'd been expecting my appearance.

"Shut the door, Fee."

I did as he said and came to stand beside him, sharing his view of the shore through the rain-spattered glass. The lighthouse seemed a world away from the warmth of the dark masculine room.

"She loved it there," he said quietly. "I warned her it was dangerous, begged her not to go. I even tried ordering her not to, but she paid me no heed. She went every day, rain or shine."

How many times had he stood here, watching her go? Had he watched her that last day, knowing it was the last time she'd go to the lighthouse? Had he slipped through the door, followed her to the top, and thrown her over? Shocked at my train of thought, I latched on to the weather and his words for another explanation of Desi's death.

"Was it raining the day she died? Is there a chance she might have slipped and fallen over the edge?"

He shook his head. "It was a beautiful, clear morning. There is a waist-high balustrade that surrounds the parapet. It would have been nearly impossible for her to stumble over it."

"Could she have jumped?" The words were harsh and bitter, but finally freed.

It broke my heart to think of my vibrant sister so desolate that she would leap to her death, but I thought again of the woman my overwrought mind had conjured up on the way to the cemetery. How happy she'd seemed as she soared upward, before the terrified realization that she was falling. Had Calvin's wife done the same?

He breathed deeply through his nose, letting the air pass from his mouth before speaking. "Perhaps you should sit down, Ophelia."

My heart pounding at the look on his face, I braced myself for what he would say.

"Just tell me, Cade. Please."

"As with everything about your sister, her death was not simple. It wasn't one that could easily be written off as an accident or a suicide." He searched my face, his eyes full of concern as his hands wrapped around my upper arms. "She was blindfolded, Fee, and her hands were tied behind her back. There's no way she could have done that to herself."

As the full impact of his words hit me, I was grateful for his hands on my arms, keeping me from falling to the floor as a strange keening sound filled the air around us. I imagined her there in the place she loved, unable to see, unable to effectively fight for her life, as someone pushed her toward the edge. I could almost hear her pleas for mercy, her screams as she was forced over the railing. Had her feet fought for purchase, had she felt the presence of the rocks as she neared them? Had she felt the immeasurable pain of her body being crushed against the jagged stones, or had she died instantly upon impact? Had she known the identity of the person who hurled her to her death? Had it been someone she loved?

These were the questions that swirled in my head, as my legs buckled and the room grew dim around me. I felt Cade's hands tighten, heard him say my name, but I could do nothing except give in to the horror of what my sister had endured. I wondered vaguely if this was the phenomena people spoke of, a supernatural connection that allowed me to feel Desdemona's terror even after she was gone. As if I were there myself, I felt the rush of wind, the way the ground rose up to meet me, and the total darkness that descended at the moment of impact.

I came back to myself slowly, aware of the sofa beneath me and a moist cloth on my forehead. I opened my eyes to see Cade kneeling beside me, his face dark with concern as he ran the wet rag over my skin. Dory stood just behind him, a basin of water in her hands and her eyes huge with fear.

"Are you okay, miss?" she asked. "You scared half the life out of me, and Mr. Cade too, I'd say."

"I'm fine, Dory," I pushed myself upright, and Cade came to his feet. He placed the cloth back in the basin.

"That will be all, Dory. Thank you." He turned back to me as she scurried from the room. "Are you sure you're all right?"

"Yes." I tried to say the word firmly, to assure him that I was not about to faint again, but it came out as a broken whisper, and was followed by an even softer denial. "No."

I promptly burst into tears, and Cade sat beside me on the settee. Without a sound, he gathered me in his arms, holding me as I wept against his solid chest. When my sobs had subsided to a point where I could talk, I pushed away and looked into his face.

"Tell me why someone would have killed my sister, Cade, and why everyone believes it was you."

"I could tell you they believe in my guilt only because I am her husband and had the most to gain from her death, but that would be a lie. It isn't simply because I was her husband. Everyone here, from the lowliest servant to the town sheriff himself, heard me threaten to kill her. Less than a week later she was dead, and all eyes turned to me."

I remained quiet, and if he was surprised by my lack of shock at his confession, he didn't show it as he continued.

"I threatened her, Fee, but I didn't kill her. There are no other suspects, however, and my guilt would prove quite fortuitous for my relatives, so there isn't a real outcry for the authorities to find another."

I waited for him to mention Amelia's suicide, to tell me that the suspicion still lingered, but he remained silent on the subject.

"What about that man Devlin?" I asked. Would the mention of Amelia's brother make him think of her? Would he tell me about her then?

"Devlin and I have known each other since our schooldays. His mutual friendship is one of the few things Calvin and I have ever had in common."

"Was he mad even then?" I asked, trying to imagine the wild-eyed man who had interrupted Desi's funeral at the kind of social functions Calvin and Cade Scott must have attended in their youth.

Cade chuckled in spite of his seriousness. "He was always a little more impassioned than the rest of us, more sensitive, some might say. He was an artist, after all, more prone to give in to emotion than logic. His flair for the dramatic was a running joke amongst us, but it drew the ladies to him like moths to a flame."

"Even Desi?" I asked softly, remembering his professions of love at her funeral.

"Most especially Desi." Cade stood and began to pace the room. Even now, as he spoke of his marriage to my sister, I couldn't help my admiration of his muscles straining against his shirt. "A year ago, we attended another schoolmate's birthday celebration and Devlin was there. The man's wife had arranged for Devlin to paint a large lifelike painting of a hunt scene as a gift to him. Devlin unveiled it there, and Desdemona fell in love with his talent instantly. She had been talking about commissioning a painting from the top of the lighthouse, and she decided right then and there that Devlin must be the one who painted it. The arrangements were made before we left that night, and he arrived at Almenara a fortnight later. From the moment he alighted from his carriage, he and my wife were inseparable."

I heard the pain in his voice and it brought my mind back to the original conversation and his motive for murder.

"Is that why you threatened to kill her?"

"No. Her affair with Devlin was only the last in several affairs Desdemona had over the years."

"Oh, Cade." It broke my heart to think of him caught up in such a web of hurt and deceit.

"I neither need nor want your pity, Ophelia. I stopped caring long ago. We are both adults, and we both know Desi never loved me. She only married me—"

Whatever he was going to say was lost as he grabbed me by the arms and hauled me against him. His pain-filled eyes searched mine for answers and truth.

"I didn't leave you for her to have."

His hands encircled my head, his lips mere inches from mine.

"It doesn't really matter, does it? None of it ever changed the way you feel in my arms, the way your eyes widen with desire when I touch you. This may be the only true thing that ever existed between any of us."

His mouth was hard and bruising, forcing a whimper from me as his hands tightened about my skull and he sought the truth from me with his kiss. I surrendered my heart and soul for his perusal, and he groaned against my mouth. His touch gentled, his lips becoming softer, but no less demanding, and I returned his passion without shame or regret.

When at last he lifted his head, he looked nearly as dazed as I felt. He cupped my face gently in his hands, and gave his head a soft shake.

Eleanor burst through the study door. Soaking wet and leached of color, she grasped the doorpost for support.

"Cade, come quickly," she panted. "There's a body on the lighthouse rocks."

He pushed past her without a word, and I slid my arms around her waist, leading her to a small chair near the door. Once she was seated, I poured her a glass of water from the pitcher on the side table and placed it in her trembling hands.

"Do you know who it is?" I asked as she gulped the water.

"The maid, Susan McCray."

I gasped in recognition of the name.

"What is it?" Eleanor asked, peering up at me.

"N-nothing," I stammered. I couldn't possibly tell her about the kiss Susan had seen or the hateful words she'd spoken at Desi's funeral.

Lorraine appeared at the door, looking quite shaken. "Eleanor, darling, are you quite all right? Calvin told me you found poor Susan's body. How horrible for you."

Eleanor latched on to Lorraine's hands, letting her sister-in-law pull her up from the chair and wrap a comforting arm around her shoulders. Without another word to me, the two of them left the room, deep in conversation.

"What in the world were you doing out there in this rain?" I heard Lorraine ask.

"I was worried for Devlin."

"Oh, Eleanor, you must let that man go."

Their voices faded away as they rounded the corner at the end of the hall.

Although I was tempted to follow them, I turned the opposite direction, toward the kitchen. I was my father's daughter, after all, and I had been raised to care for the needs of the grieving.

"What utter nonsense, Kathleen," Mrs. Hartley was saying as I slipped into the kitchen.

A dark-haired girl of about sixteen was seated by the fire, and the eyes of everyone in the room were fixed on her as she spoke, "I swear I heard it, Mrs. Hartley. Crying like I've never heard before. It was an omen, I tell you. An omen that something bad was to happen. Like Mrs. Scott herself come back to warn us. If only Susan would have listened."

The short round cook looked up from the stew she was stirring as she listened to the girl's tale. Her tearstained face registered surprise when she caught sight of me.

"Miss Garrett. Can I get you something?"

A collective gasp escaped several of the maids as every eye turned toward me. There were varying degrees of grief and fear on their faces, and I wondered what they would think if I confirmed Kathleen's story. Although I firmly doubted it was Desdemona returned from the grave, I had no other explanation for the crying I had heard every night since my arrival.

"No, thank you. I heard about Susan, and I wanted to see if there was anything I could do to help. Does she have family?"

It was quite possible she had a husband and

children; at the very least she would probably have a mother and father who would be grief-stricken at the news of her death. The thought of the gruff and angry Calvin Scott acting as the sheriff and giving someone such news was hard for me to comprehend. Perhaps those things were left to Reverend Arnold, although he was so reserved, it was very nearly as difficult for me to imagine him as a comforting shoulder to lean upon.

"I used to go with my father to comfort families who had lost loved ones. Will Reverend Arnold go to them? Or will Sheriff Scott himself tell them?"

Mrs. Hartley spoke from her place beside the fire.

"Her sister is married to one of the groomsmen, Tom Shelton. We've already sent them home to deliver the news to her parents."

Her usually kind eyes did not welcome me to linger, and I nodded in agreement. I was, after all, not a servant or even the local vicar's daughter. Here at Almenara, I was one of the family. "Please let me know if there is anything I can do for them."

"Of course, Miss Garrett. Thank you."

"Not like her sister at all," one of the maids remarked dryly as I stepped into the hall. The door closed on the murmur of agreement that rippled through the room.

Chapter Twelve

As soon as I left the kitchen, I pulled on my cloak and headed to the dunes behind the house. There had been a brief lull in the rain, but as I neared the place where a rocky path led over the edge of the dunes to the shore below, the skies opened up again and I was quickly drenched through.

The wind caught at my skirts and cloak, whipping them around my legs. My hair escaped from its pins and several wisps came from beneath the cloak to slap loosely about my face.

I could see nothing ahead of me except a wall of rain, and I stopped, afraid I would lose my footing and slide down the dune.

"What the devil are you doing out here?" Cade bellowed as he appeared on the path before me. He and three other men carried a shrouded bundle between them, and I knew it contained the battered body of Susan McCray.

I hadn't the faintest idea what I was doing there, except for the morbid curiosity that drew me to see firsthand the place where my sister had been murdered days ago, and another pretty young woman had now met her own demise,

The question on my own mind was whether she had met it by accident or intent.

"Get back to the house!" His voice brooked no

argument, but I shook my head, ignoring his command as I moved forward. The rain came down in sheets, biting into my face and hands with icy precision, but I pressed on, determined to finally gaze upon the rocks where Desi had died.

Cade shouted something at me about breaking my fool neck, but knowing he couldn't stop me at the moment, I hurried on.

I picked my way over numerous rocks of varying sizes, and when I finally stood directly under the shadow of the lighthouse, the larger rocks that created a barrier between earth and sea blocked my path. Even in the pouring rain, I could see the tint of blood upon them, turning the water pink as it washed past them on its way back to the sea.

I shuddered with horror and hurried away from the water, toward the open door of the lighthouse. Above me, I could hear the voices of the men who were investigating Susan's death. I strained to hear them as I entered, but it wasn't until I was halfway up the stairs that their words became clear.

"Same as before," one said.

"Cade got any reason to want this one dead?" the other clucked, and I cringed at the thought. He hadn't been happy at her sly innuendoes during Desi's funeral, but I hardly believed he would see that as motive enough to kill her.

I continued upward, intent on protesting their suspicions, but someone rushed past me, pushing me out of the way, and my feet lost their purchase. My head collided with the brick wall as I went down, and spots danced before my eyes.

For the second time that day, I opened my eyes to

find myself lying on my back with Cade holding a cloth to my head. My vision was blurry, but I struggled to rise.

"Lie still, Fee," Dennis Ames said, pressing a hand against my shoulder. His deep green eyes were dark with concern. "The doctor is on his way."

"I'm fine," I protested, but I didn't fight against either his or Cade's grip, as I knew my weak attempts would prove futile against their combined strength. I felt bruised from head to toe, and my temple throbbed with pain.

"You're not fine." Cade's declaration was choked with some emotion I suspected was anger. "What in the world were you thinking? I told you to go home. Those steps are a hazard at the best of times, and with the rain, and everyone coming in and out, they're wet and slick as ice. If Dennis hadn't been behind you and stopped your descent, you'd have tumbled all the way down the stairs."

I reached up and touched my head gingerly, shocked by the blood that smeared my fingertips. "I'm bleeding?"

"You probably hit your head when you fell," Dennis explained. "You were out cold when I caught you and carried you down."

"Someone ran into me and I hit my head on the wall."

"No one hit you, Ophelia." I turned my face toward Cade's icy stare.

"I'm sure it was an accident, Cade, and I shouldn't have been in the way, but I know what happened."

"That knock on your head has you confused, Fee," Dennis offered. "There was no one on the stairs but me and you. Maybe a piece of plaster or a stone fell from the wall. I didn't see or hear one hit, but it could have, all the same."

Cade scrubbed a hand across his face but was kept from commenting when the doctor called out to us from the top of the dunes. Without a word, Cade scooped me into his arms and stalked through the rain toward the house.

"Thank you, Dennis," I said to the young man trailing behind us.

"No problem, Fee. Glad I could be of service."

He tipped his dripping hat my way before hurrying toward Calvin and a group of men who stood around the open wagon carrying the shrouded remains of Susan McCray. A small sound of dismay escaped me as it dawned on me how close I might have come to joining her there.

Cade didn't speak, but his arms tightened around me, holding me even closer to his chest, and making me wonder if he was thinking the same thing.

Within minutes of Cade depositing me in my room, Richard had stitched up my head wound, diagnosed a concussion and multiple bruises, and inquired if I was out of my mind for going outside in such weather. I had expected a little more sympathy from him, I suppose, for his question irritated me quite thoroughly.

Before leaving, he gave Cade a small bottle of laudanum, accompanied by orders that I rest for several days.

"She'll need this for pain. It will also help her rest. If you give her a healthy dose each night and again at noon, we shouldn't have to worry about her dashing off on any more wild goose chases for a while."

Cade walked the doctor downstairs and, although I tried to wait for his return, I eventually succumbed to the drowsiness caused by both my injury and the dose of medicine Richard had already administered.

Chapter Thirteen

I woke hours later. The thin light of the moon shone through the windows and my bedroom door, which stood slightly ajar. I remembered it closing behind Cade when he left the room, and I wondered if he, Dory, or even one of his relatives, had peeked in on their way to bed. My head and body ached and I gingerly touched the bandage on my forehead. Had I only imagined that someone hit me? Although I was certain I had felt someone push past me, it was possible I had simply slipped on the wet stone and fallen forward, or as Dennis surmised, a piece of the crumbling wall hit me and caused me to fall. Since Dennis swore no one had come up or down the stairs past him, I had no choice but to accept these as the only possible explanations.

The now familiar sound of weeping drifted through the open door, and I slid from my bed and tiptoed closer. The crying was quieter tonight, and as I pushed open the door, I thought I heard the soft coo of a mourning dove. I scanned the darkened hallway and stopped short at the sight of the girl standing at the window. The moon coming through the glass cast an ethereal glow over the white cloak that covered her head and shoulders. Her hands were cupped around a small gray dove and, as I had seen my sister do many times as a girl, she brought it to her lips for a soft kiss on its head, before setting it gently on the windowsill in front of the open window

"Desi?" I whispered, my heart leaping with joy even as my head told me it was madness.

At the sound of my voice, the girl turned and fled, past the staircase and down the opposite hallway.

"Wait!" I cried, running after her. She pulled open the door at the end of the hall and darted up the stairs to the roof. "Wait!"

I didn't even think about my fear of heights when I dashed up the stairs behind her, and only stopped halfway across the roof when I realized she was nowhere in sight.

I barely registered the sound of running feet as the household responded to my cries.

Suddenly, Cade was beside me, demanding an explanation as he dragged me back into the hallway, where the servants who had rushed upstairs to defend me stood in a frightened group. I had no idea whether they were frightened for me or of me.

"What happened?" Cade questioned again, and I looked up at him.

"Nothing," I said, unwilling to share this experience with anyone until I had time to examine it myself.

"What do you mean, nothing? You seem to be as hell-bent on falling to your death as your sister was."

"Cade," Mrs. Hartley gasped, and I wondered if I was the only one who noticed her omission of his title.

At her reprimand, he spun around and faced the small group. "You may all go back to your beds. Everything appears to be fine."

They dispersed quickly, if somewhat reluctantly,

each one daring a curious glance at the door through which my ghostly visitor had disappeared. I pushed past Cade and went to the windows. Thinking I might see some hint of the girl there, I scanned the empty courtyard below. There was no sign of her, no visible way for her to have made it off the roof.

With a heavy sigh, I started back toward my room, Cade following with his arms crossed in disapproval.

As I passed the window where the dove had been, I leaned out, certain I would find it somewhere on the veranda. Again, there was nothing there, and within seconds Cade's hand closed about my arm and forced me to continue on.

Once inside, he pushed the door closed and motioned to the bed.

"Get in bed."

I shook my head. I would not be spoken to like a child, and I most certainly would not obey him as if I were one.

"I think I'll sit up and read for a while." I sounded just like a petulant child.

"Ophelia, the doctor instructed you to stay in bed. I can't imagine what you were doing on the roof, but you are still recovering from one fall and seem to want to push your luck with another."

"Someone was at the window, Cade. She left a little bird there. I chased her down the other hall, but she disappeared on the roof."

"What? Who?"

"I don't know. I heard the crying, and the coo of a dove, so I went out to the hallway. She was standing there holding it. I saw her."

He shook his head. "Perhaps it was the laudanum

Richard gave you. I will speak to him tomorrow about the possibility that the medication induced hallucinations, or sleepwalking accompanied by a vivid nightmare."

"I was not hallucinating! And I most certainly was not sleepwalking!"

"That is the only explanation, Ophelia. There was no sign of a woman on the rooftop or a bird in the hallway. The courtyard and the veranda were completely empty."

"The servants say the house is haunted."

"What does that have to do with anything?" Comprehension dawned on his face and he stared at me in surprise. "You think you saw a ghost?"

I wasn't really sure what I thought. I still couldn't quite fathom a ghostly encounter, but I was having a harder and harder time convincing myself that the crying woman was anything else.

"My levelheaded, calm Ophelia thinks she saw a ghost?" he asked again, a smile playing about his mouth. I wanted to slap him, but I had never given in to violence and refused to do so now.

"Did you know my father called me his little mourning dove and Desi his barn swallow? She always loved birds so. We would go out after a storm to look for nests that had fallen from the trees so that she could raise the abandoned baby birds. When the birds were big enough, she always let them go the same way. She would kiss them on the head, and then put them on the windowsill and wait for them to fly away. That's what the girl in the hall did."

"You think it was Desdemona's ghost you saw? Really?" He did smile this time, and with gentle hands, he pressed me toward the bed. "Lie down, Fee."

Tears burned my throat as I remembered lying beneath the apple tree in our father's yard while Desi climbed to the highest branch possible. Had Desi been unhappy even then? Had she already felt the stirring of wildness inside her? Had she ever thought of casting herself to the ground where I lay? Had the future haunted her as the past did me?

"There's a good girl," Cade soothed, and I was surprised to find that I was lying back on my bed. He pulled the covers up over my chest and bent to place a soft kiss on my forehead. "You need to rest."

Panic seized me, and before he could move away, my arms encircled his neck.

"Don't leave me, Cade," I heard myself say, fear causing my voice to quaver.

Dark eyes met mine, delved their depths and then softened with understanding. "I won't leave you, Fee, but I can't stay here in your bed."

He gently extricated himself from my arms and turned toward the bedside table.

I watched him fill a spoon with medication and hold it out to me. I knew he was right, he couldn't stay in my bed, but I didn't care about propriety at the moment. Except for the kisses he and I had shared since my arrival, it had been years since I had been held in even the most innocent of ways.

Although my father had been somewhat lost in his own world, his arms were always open for either of his daughters, and I had grown up knowing I was loved. When I met Cade, I had been a girl confident in her youth and worth, certain I would find a man who would love me as my father had so obviously loved my mother. Now, here I was, a woman alone in the world and unsure of her worth as anything other than Reverend Garrett's spinster daughter. In the past, I had rarely allowed myself the luxury of self-pity or restlessness. I had accepted my fate and made the best of it by serving the people in my community and remaining active at the church my father had ministered in for so many years.

Since my arrival at Almenara, however, the need to be more was becoming increasingly unbearable. I wanted this man to love me, to take me to the places our hearts had only hinted at all those years ago. It no longer mattered that my sister had been there before, that he had loved her, bedded her, and made her his wife. I would be content to be his second choice, to be the one who took her place.

At least, that is what I told myself.

"Drink it," he said. I started to shake my head, but he put the spoon to my lips and murmured again, "Drink it."

Once I had, he pulled a chair up beside my bed and sat down. He was silent as he took my hand in his and began to trace the lines of it with one finger. By the time he spoke, my body had relaxed and my eyelids were beginning to droop.

"Do you remember how it was with us, Fee?" His voice was soft and wistful.

"Yes." Of course I remembered how it was. No matter how I struggled to forget, I had always remembered. It had to be the drug that made me admit, "I remember it every day."

"I loved you from the moment I saw you," he said, bringing my hand to his lips.

I forced my eyes open, fighting the laudanum-induced haze that was quickly descending on me.

"You quit the moment I was out of your sight."

He lifted dark, haunted eyes to mine. "I never quit, Fee. Not for a minute."

Chapter Fourteen

I greeted the next morning with a pounding headache and stiff limbs, but with a new sense of determination that refused to be deterred by the pain. If I was being haunted by Desdemona's ghost, then there had to be a reason she would not move on to the next world. I reminded myself more than once that I didn't believe in ghosts or other paranormal beings, and that it was most likely my unresolved relationship with my sister that was causing me to conjure up such unearthly happenings. Still, I was so certain the things I had seen and heard were real, it was impossible to convince myself they were the workings of my mind, no matter how disturbed my thoughts.

I dressed for church in a solemn black dress and twisted my hair into its usual chignon. As an afterthought, I pinned a small dove-shaped brooch made of silver and gum-paste jewels to my bodice. It wasn't suitable for mourning, but I didn't care. It was a reminder of happier times when Desi and I had still lived as sisters under our father's roof. The brooch had been a gift from my father on my sixteenth birthday. He had given Desi one in the shape of a swallow. Purchased from a merchant during one of his infrequent trips into the city, my father had claimed I was like the dove who found its nourishment close to the ground and Desi was like the swallow who took to the sky in search of sustenance. It was as poetic as I ever heard my father wax outside of his sermons, and I could almost hear his voice now as I studied my reflection in the mirror.

I wondered idly if Desi had kept hers all these years and if she had ever worn it as a reminder of fond memories and familial ties.

I was waiting downstairs when Cade came down dressed in a well-cut dark suit, his hair still damp from a morning bath. My breath caught in my throat as I watched him descend, his proclamation of the night before ringing in my head.

Lorraine, Calvin, and Eleanor were directly behind him, their Sunday best reminding me that beside them in the family pew I would look like the poor country relation I was. Instead of making me feel self-conscious and unsure, however, the knowledge seemed to bolster me, reminding me of my place in the world and here at Almenara. No matter what else I was or would ever be, I was first and foremost a woman whom others trusted and looked to for comfort, aid, and advice. I had sat by my father's side while he took his dying breath, and I would be at Cade's side when he took his, if it all came to that. In the meantime, I would do whatever I could to help prove his innocence.

When he saw me up and dressed, Cade glared at me for only a moment before offering me his arm and leading me to the waiting carriage.

"I expect that you plan to rest once the services are over?" he inquired and ordered simultaneously, unable to keep his disapproval in check.

"Of course," I agreed, although I truthfully had little intention of lying about all day.

"Are you sure you're up to this, Ophelia?" Eleanor asked. "I'm certain the Lord would forgive your absence from church service while you're recovering from your fall."

"I am certain He would, but I am looking forward to hearing Reverend Arnold preach. Aside from a little stiffness and an ache here and there, I appear to be fine."

"She will rest this afternoon and tomorrow," Cade announced, and I shot him a look of annoyance at the heavy-handed edict.

When we reached the church in the center of town, Calvin, Lorraine, and Eleanor exited the vehicle and made their way up the stone path, acknowledging the greetings of the villagers with nods and smiles. By the time Cade and I alighted, they were well ahead of us, and I wondered at their hurry. I didn't wonder long as I looked around at the faces of the people who had just greeted them so kindly. To a man, they eyed Cade with thinly veiled distrust and suspicion.

Wanting to offer him more in the way of encouragement than simply standing by his side, I slipped my hand into the crook of his arm. He placed his other hand on mine and gave it a gentle squeeze as we approached the door.

"She was screaming like a banshee, I tell you. I heard her with my own ears. Desdemona raised from the grave and trying to warn the rest of us, I'd bet." My eyes shot to the group of girls enraptured by young Kathleen's rendition of the story I'd overheard in the kitchen after Susan's body was found. I couldn't help but notice that she now used Desdemona's first name rather than calling her Mrs. Scott. I supposed it had a

117

much more dramatic ring to it when told that way.

Some of the girls caught me looking at them, and glanced away, ashamed to be caught gossiping, but the others simply leaned in closer as Kathleen continued.

"Her sister's seen it, too. No one's said so, of course, but I saw it on her face last night. She screamed out Desdemona's name, and we all came running. When we got to her, she was pale as a ghost herself and standing out on the roof of Almenara."

"That's enough, Kathleen!" an older woman said, grabbing her by the arm and pulling her away. She had the same dark hair and eyes as the storyteller, and I guessed it was Kathleen's mother even before the woman spoke to us. "Pardon my girl, Mr. Scott, miss, we've not yet been able to beat the imagination out of her."

I opened my mouth to protest such harsh punishment for girlish talk, but Cade tightened his grip on my hand and, after a nod to Kathleen's mother, led me inside the church. We slipped into the pew beside Dennis Ames and in front of the rest of the Scott family just as the pianist began to play.

Dennis leaned toward me and spoke in a rather loud whisper. "I'm surprised to see you here, Fee. I thought the doctor would have ordered you to rest."

I was spared answering by Richard himself, who slid into the pew on the other side of Dennis. "That's exactly what the doctor ordered. Yet here she is. At least she's not likely to get in trouble inside the church."

"She will rest when we return home," Cade said from my other side, without even looking our way, and I rolled my eyes in what I'm sure was a very unladylike expression.

****

Reverend Arnold proved to be just as mild-mannered a preacher as he was a man, and I had to fight to keep my mind engaged in his sermon. The high point of the service was a benediction sung by Nellie Arnold in a high, lilting soprano that would make an angel proud.

Afterward, we had barely made it through the front door of Almenara before Cade was ordering me to my room to rest, promising he'd have a lunch tray sent up momentarily. Although I disliked his assumption that I would blindly obey his commands, I offered only superficial protests. The truth was I wanted to be alone without his watchful eyes while I thought about what my next move should be. My mind had worked feverishly throughout the church service, and I had a fairly clear idea of where I needed to go next. I just needed directions on how to get there.

A knock on the door interrupted my thoughts, and Dory came through the door carrying a tray. Cade was just behind her, a tray in his hand, as well. My surprise and disappointment must have shown on my face, for he gave me a somewhat uncertain smile as Dory left the room.

"I hope you won't mind my company," he said as he removed items from the tray and set them on the table. "For some reason, I find myself dreading a formal family meal today."

I watched him closely as he readied the meal, and we settled in front of the window. For the first time, I noticed the worry that furrowed his brow, the deep lines that bracketed his mouth, and the sad weariness in his eyes. Tears of sympathy sprang to my eyes, and I dashed them away with my fingers.

He began to eat, giving no indication that he had noticed my perusal or tears, and I followed suit as he began to talk.

"I've had the guardianship paperwork drawn up, and it should be delivered before the end of the week. Despite what I told Lorraine and Calvin, I have never had any intention of leaving Tabitha in their care. Although I don't fear for her safety with them, I do fear that she would be deprived of the love and care she deserves."

"Why do they want her so badly? Is there something they stand to gain?" I felt uncharitable even asking such a question, but both Mrs. Hartley's and Lorraine's words came back to me, and I wondered if Cade was being naive to think she wasn't in danger from his family.

"No, there is nothing for them to gain. At one time, there may have been motive for them to harm her, if they were those kinds of people, which I don't believe them to be. But the condition of my release prior to the trial was that I signed papers surrendering Almenara and everything it entails to Calvin, effective immediately, should I be found guilty of murder."

I gasped and sat back in my seat.

"Cade, how could you do such a thing?"

"I wanted to be home, Fee. I didn't want to spend the last weeks of my life alone, locked up in a jail cell. I wanted to spend them here with Tabby, and God help me, Fee, with you."

His voice cracked and he buried his face in his hands.

I knelt on the floor beside his chair, wrapping my arms around his shoulders and pulling him against me, holding him as sadness and fear rolled over us in great waves.

Of its own accord our embrace became something else and he lifted love-starved lips to my own. It wasn't until our kisses deepened to a need we could not satisfy without ramifications that we broke apart.

"Why did you marry her, Cade?" I whispered breathlessly. I had waited for him to come for me. I could still remember the days turning to weeks, the weeks to months, until finally I received the telegram telling me he and Desi had married. I could see the refusal on his face, but I needed to have an answer. "I deserve an answer, Cade. You betrayed me, you broke my heart, and you brought my sister here to die. I want to know why."

"You know exactly why, Ophelia." His eyes were ice-cold onyx, devoid of the passion that lit them moments before. "I did exactly what you expected. Fell into the trap the two of you laid."

"What?" Had he lost his mind?

"Don't pretend you don't know what I'm talking about." He grabbed me by the arms and growled, "I was doomed the moment she stepped foot off that boat."

"Cade, I—"

"I can still hear you begging me to look after her, to be her friend. I still feel your sobs the night before you left, and taste your lips when we kissed that last time. Even these years later, I had hoped it was unintentional, that you somehow didn't know she was pregnant. That it wasn't all an elaborate scheme to make me think I was the father of her child." His voice shook with fury and pain. "But now I know. You chose to leave."

I could barely breathe as I stared at him, stunned by his accusations and revelation. Desi had been pregnant? And she had used Cade to cover it up? How could I not have known? Why hadn't she told me? Because she knew I would never agree to such a hoax. If I hadn't left her with Cade, she would have found another man to dupe. But Cade had been handy, and obviously it hadn't been very difficult for her to sway him into bedding her.

"She had been carrying on with a married man," I choked out. "A preacher, no less, and my father was devastated when he learned of their affair. He threw her out of the house and told her not to return. She was so ill on the trip to New Orleans, so weak and sick when she arrived, that I wasn't sure she could withstand the return journey."

My voice broke, but I continued, desperate to make him believe me.

"I had no idea she was pregnant, Cade. You have to believe that. I thought it was only nerves and worry that made her so ill. I hoped that by the time Father recovered, he would be ready to forgive her and let her come home. It never occurred to me that she would take my place in your affections."

"Damn it, Ophelia, she never took your place."

"You married her, Cade, not me. You believed her child was yours."

He ran an agitated hand through his hair.

"You begged me to look after her, Fee, to be a friend to her, and that's what I did. She was so like you, at first, so sweet and caring. Your sister had acting abilities that rivaled Lorraine's, I'm sure. Those first few weeks after you were gone, she was so like you it was as if I had a living, breathing portrait of you at my side. Her smile, her laugh, even her demeanor was the same. Quite truthfully, I did become nearly as enamored with her as I was with you." He darted a glance out the window. "There were differences in you, of course. As time passed, she became more and more brazen in her desire for physical intimacy. I suppose she knew time was running out for her to claim her child was mine. By the time we crossed that line, she must have already been several months along."

"So you believed she was pregnant with your child when you married her?"

He nodded. "Tabby was such a frail little thing when she was born, it was easy to tell myself she was weeks early. I loved her from the moment I laid eyes on her. No child could have been more precious to me."

His voice was thick with emotion, and my eyes welled with tears. There was no doubt in my mind that he loved Tabby like his own.

"I wasn't prepared for the protectiveness and love I felt for her when they placed her in my arms. I knew right away that something wasn't right with her, that she was different from other babies, but it didn't matter. It only made the feelings stronger."

"How did you learn she wasn't really your child?"

"Maybe I always knew. In the back of my mind, I had my doubts, but I forced myself to keep them there. I knew I wasn't the first for Desdemona, and, in retrospect, I knew that Tabitha's birth was too early for her to have survived, had she been mine. But none of that mattered to me. I wanted to believe she was my daughter. We could have gone on like that forever, but Desdemona kept taking her up to the top of that damn lighthouse. Richard kept warning her it was dangerous, but she refused to listen. Finally, he came to me with his concerns."

"He told me how dangerous it was for her to be there," I said, and Cade shot me a look of dark disapproval.

"Desdemona and I fought about it. She was furious and spat out that Tabby wasn't mine and I had no right to tell her what she could do with her. She threatened to divorce me and take Tabitha away. I denied her a divorce, and she vowed to leave anyway. I was so angry that I threatened to kill her if she ever tried to take Tabby with her. And everyone heard me say it." He clasped my hand, his face shadowed with regret. "I meant it when I said it, Fee. It's important that you know that."

"Cade, you were angry, and frightened by her threats to take the child you love. That isn't proof you killed her."

"It's proof enough, apparently."

"Do you think she would really have left?"

"Yes, I think she had every intention of leaving. I'm not sure she would have taken Tabby, but she and Devlin had every intention of leaving the country. He'd already booked passage on a ship to England."

"She really loved him that much?"

"With Devlin, she was different than I had ever seen her. I suspected she had taken a lover here and there during our marriage, but she was always discreet. She and I had ceased having a real marital relationship long ago, but I suppose some affection for her still remained within me, because I was almost glad to see her happy once more. Devlin was more than an affair. I believe Devlin was the one man your sister ever truly loved."

"Did he return her love?" Everything I had learned since coming to Almenara painted such a bleak picture of Desi's life here, it seemed imperative that I know if she had found any sort of happiness in the end.

He nodded. "Even without his dramatic tendencies, what you saw at her funeral was real. Devlin loved her."

"But you can't say for sure he didn't kill her?"

"No."

I knew I needed to ask him about Amelia while he was so willing to talk. Although I couldn't really believe he'd had anything to do with her death, I had to know what had transpired between them the day she died, and what part her death played in his arrest for Desi's murder.

I took a deep breath. "Tell me about Amelia."

He paled, swallowed hard, and with what appeared to be supreme effort, spoke in a voice I barely recognized.

"Amelia and Calvin married the year he graduated. Calvin and I had spent holidays with Devlin at their parents' home, and they seemed to care for us. But when Calvin proposed, they became vocal in their disapproval of the match. They wanted more for her, wanted her to marry someone who would be able to care for her, who could make her the mistress of her own home. It seems they had decided she would be mistress of Almenara or she would not live here at all."

For the first time, I saw why Calvin envied Cade,

why his dislike was so palpable. At every turn, it seemed Cade was chosen over him.

"Amelia and Calvin married against her parents' wishes, and Calvin lavished her with all the things her parents had not expected him to be able to give her. Despite the costs, he determined to make her life as grand as possible. We fought over their expenditures constantly, and the last day of her life, we came to blows in the courtyard."

"Oh, my."

"We were young and hotheaded, and neither of us cared about anything but proving our point." He stood up and moved to the window. "By the time we stopped fighting, she was gone. Once I cooled down, I felt badly about the things I said, and I wanted to apologize, but she was nowhere to be found. We searched for her and I happened upon her at the top of the lighthouse. She was hysterical, and I tried to calm her, but she climbed up on the railing."

He dug a long-fingered hand through his dark hair and breathed deeply. "I tried to stop her. I moved closer, praying she wouldn't notice, praying I could catch her and pull her down to safety. But she was so determined, so quick. I tried to reach her, but all I caught was the edge of her petticoat. When I came down, Calvin was there beside her body and I held nothing but a bit of white satin in my hand."

"Excuse me, Mr. Cade. Mr. Calvin is demanding your presence downstairs immediately," Mrs. Hartley said from the doorway.

"It seems I've become a suspect in yet another murder," he explained, his eyes and face expressionless. "I assume it's time for me to answer a few questions."

Chapter Fifteen

Despite Cade's inexplicable acceptance of their suspicion, my own mind and heart refused to accept that he could be responsible for one death, much less three, and my resolve to prove his innocence strengthened. For the first time in years, hope for the future beat in my chest, and I longed to believe that Cade and I would face that future together.

The days were quickly passing, however, and a week from now Cade would be taken to the jail to await his trial for Desi's murder. It would be a very brief trial, based on what everyone considered to be an open-and-shut case, and in all likelihood it would end with Cade's hanging. A cold empty pit formed in my stomach at the thought, and I groaned in frustration.

I could not stand idly by and watch Cade die for a crime I knew in my heart he didn't commit. If no one else cared enough to look for another explanation for Desdemona's death, then it was up to me, and I had decided that my first contact should be with Devlin. He was obviously key to my understanding Desdemona's death, as well as to the life she'd lived here at Almenara.

Dory entered the room just as I finished lacing up my walking boots.

"Good afternoon," I said as she bobbed a curtsy and began to clear our lunch away.

"Afternoon, miss. Mister Cade said you were to rest for the rest of the afternoon. You already went against the doctor's orders going to church this morning."

"To my knowledge, sitting in church has never done a body any harm, Dory," I told her as I finished with my shoes. I ignored the dull pain the motion of standing caused my body, and, smoothing my hand over my skirts, I shrugged nonchalantly. "Cade must have misunderstood. I feel fine this afternoon, and I've decided to go for a little walk."

"I suppose a stroll around the garden wouldn't hurt you," she said. "It's a pretty day, and there's benches around, should you get tired. Would you like me to fetch Mr. Cade? His meeting with the others is over, and he might like to accompany you."

"No!" My voice was much sharper than I intended, and I offered her a reassuring smile. "I think I may walk a little farther than the garden, and I'm sure Cade has enough to keep him busy today."

"Do you plan to take quite a long walk, then?"

"I don't know. That's what I need you to tell me."

"What?" she asked cautiously, looking at me as if I were an escaped lunatic she wasn't quite sure how to handle.

"Do you have any idea where I might find Devlin?"

"Devlin, miss?"

"Yes, the man who painted the picture in Desdemona's parlor. The man who interrupted her funeral. Does he live nearby?"

"I don't know, miss. He stayed here when he was painting. After him and Mr. Calvin had it out, he left."

"Calvin?" I repeated. Did that man drive everyone to fisticuffs?

"I wasn't there to witness it, but according to my brother, Mr. Calvin beat the living daylights out of Devlin and sent him packing."

"And you haven't any idea where he went after that?"

"No, miss." Dory shook her head for good measure, but I knew her answer was far from true.

Turning her back to me, she began to fuss with the lunch leftovers. I said nothing as I pinned my bonnet in place and pulled on my gloves.

"Well then, I'll find him myself. Have a good afternoon, Dory."

As I'd hoped it would, Dory's characteristic candor won out before I could pull the door open.

"There's a cabin beyond the cemetery and lighthouse, miss, but you shouldn't go there. Mr. Cade won't like it a bit."

"Thank you, Dory."

"If you give me a note, I'll have Donald, my brother, take it there. He'll deliver a message to Devlin for you. You can have that man meet you somewhere in the village." She wrung her hands, twisting them together nervously as she second-guessed the wisdom of giving me the information. "Please, miss. Mr. Cade will be furious if you go."

I had no desire to anger Cade or cause Dory any trouble, but I didn't want to meet Devlin in the village. I didn't want to wait, and I didn't want to risk Cade finding out I was attempting to talk to him.

"Perhaps that would be a better idea," I agreed, although I had no intention of letting go of my original plan.

"So, you'll write a note for Donald to deliver?" she asked hopefully.

"I'll think about it." I'd always had difficulty lying, and with Dory's relief so evident, I found it impossible to tell her an outright lie. I would think about it as I walked, and perhaps I would change my mind about going to see Devlin unannounced. I doubted it, but there was always a chance.

I slipped down the backstairs through the kitchen, knowing that if I ran into Cade I'd have a battle on my hands. He wouldn't agree with my assessment of the doctor's orders. He appeared to think the doctor had ordered a healthy dose of laudanum every few hours and several days in bed, while I chose to interpret the doctor's orders to mean that treatment depended upon how I felt. Truthfully, my body protested every movement, but I couldn't rest until I'd spoken to Devlin.

Following the narrow road we'd taken the day of Desi's funeral, I skirted the village and went up to the hill where the church and cemetery were perched. I was through the churchyard and opening the gate to the cemetery when I heard Nellie Arnold call to me.

"Yoo-hoo, Ophelia!" She was hurrying across the yard from the parsonage behind the church, and I cursed myself for not thinking to avoid it. Dressed in the loose pink confection of billowing ruffles and rosettes she'd been wearing at the service this morning, Nellie was so far removed from any pastor's wife I had ever known as to be almost comical.

I wondered if my own mother had been more like Nellie or the quiet, staid women my father's colleagues had wed. My father had rarely spoken of her, so what I knew of her had come piecemeal from that little he'd said, Mrs. Dupree's barely concealed contempt of her, and the names she'd bestowed on her daughters. Something about Nellie reminded me of the picture those scraps of information had formed for me, and I wondered if this was why I found myself so drawn to the woman.

I met Nellie halfway across her yard, but she was still panting from exertion as she sank to the bench beneath a large shade tree. She chuckled and fanned herself with her hand.

"I've become a great lug, out of breath at even the smallest movement." When she'd caught her breath, she looked at me intently. "How are you? We heard about your fall yesterday. I must say I'm surprised to see you up and about so soon."

"I'm feeling fine and saw no reason to lie about all day. That isn't something I'm used to doing."

"No, of course not. With midnight births and break-of-dawn final passages, short nights and early mornings are the normal way of things for women who care for men of the cloth. My James tries to sneak out without waking me, but I'm a light sleeper, so he doesn't often succeed."

"My father made people feel so welcome in our home we often had visitors well into the night. Prayer services could extend until the wee hours of the morning or begin hours before daylight. Since I was the hostess, it was up to me to make everyone comfortable for as long as they were there."

"Didn't you share those duties with your sister?"

"No, Desi never took to domestic or pastoral skills

like I did."

"So, you were Martha and she was Mary? You were busy working while she was worshiping?"

"To be honest, except for her mandatory attendance at church services, she never really took to that aspect of our lives either."

"So what did she do?"

"If it was the middle of the night, she stayed in bed. If it was daytime, she went to our room, took a walk, or went into town."

"She shared your faith, though?"

"I really don't know." I was ashamed to admit the truth. I had regularly spoken to my father's parishioners about their faith, but it had been many years since I spoke to Desi of such things. As I remembered those long-ago conversations, I couldn't say for sure whether Desi had really believed as I did or not.

Nellie placed a comforting hand on my arm. "She was raised in church, Ophelia. She sat through your father's sermons the same as you. No matter about the years in between, she had that knowledge of the Lord, and we can only hope that she called on Him at the end."

Tears clogged my throat, and I nodded, unable to speak as I got control of my emotions.

"Were you headed up to visit her grave this afternoon? I apologize for detaining you, but James has been called away to attend to Mrs. Morgan. You wouldn't have met her yet. She's a dear old woman who's facing her end days and wanted James there when she spoke to her children about her last wishes. Anyway, I was feeling a bit lonely, and I was thrilled to see you crossing the yard."

"It's no problem at all. I could use a friend myself. As I'm sure you've noticed, the residents of Almenara aren't the friendliest bunch."

She laughed. "I would say not. You must miss Desdemona terribly."

"I do, but I have missed her for quite a long time now. Desdemona and I hadn't spoken in years."

"Oh, dear. I can't imagine not speaking to my sister. Although we don't see each other as often as I'd like, we are quite close even now. I can't imagine what would tear us apart."

As I had no explanation but the truth for our estrangement, I said nothing. I wasn't sure whether Nellie realized my reticence or not, but I was grateful when she went ahead with our conversation.

"It's easy to see that you and Desdemona were quite different. I can imagine that over the years, you disagreed on quite a few things. I'm sure you both had every intention of reconciling, and I'm sorry you never got that chance."

Once again, I felt the prick of tears, and shook my head ruefully. "You say you've become a great lug, and I seem to have become a leaking spigot since my arrival."

She laughed and patted my arm.

"Well, in the interest of my own transformation into a great lug, I must have some refreshment. I have an apple pie that should be cool by now. Would you care for some?"

I was about to refuse, but before I could, Devlin emerged from the woods just inside the cemetery fence. He still wore the cloak Lorraine had claimed was hers, his hair was ruffled and stood on end as if he habitually

133

ran a hand through it, and I tried to reconcile him to the picture of a gentlemen that Cade had painted of him. It was nearly impossible for me to imagine him as Cade's friend, much less my sister's lover.

I stiffened as he neared, but Nellie pushed herself to her feet with a groan and smiled.

"Devlin, how nice to see you," she said, holding her hands out to him. He took them in his and bent to kiss her cheek.

"Nellie, darling, you look lovely this morning." His voice was low, cultured, and surprisingly sane. When he turned toward me, his face was illuminated by the bright morning sunlight, and I was once again aware of his masculine beauty. Blue eyes sparkled with enthusiasm as he bowed at the waist. "Ophelia, it's good to see you here. I have been hoping to speak with you."

"We were just going in for some pie. Would you care to join us?" Nellie asked.

His eyes darted toward the road that led to the village and Almenara beyond it.

"Are you alone, Ophelia?"

"Yes, of course." My stomach fluttered with nervousness at the thought of sitting across the table from him.

"Then, yes, I would love to join you."

We followed Nellie into her cluttered kitchen. She pulled plates from the cabinet and asked me to cut the pie as she put the teakettle on to boil.

My hands shook slightly as I sliced through the pie, feeling Devlin's eyes on me the entire time. Did he realize he was the cause of my nervousness? By the time we were all seated, I could do little more than pick at my pie as he continued his silent perusal. Finally, he sighed and sat back in his chair.

"I find it hard to believe you and she are so different."

"I'm sure in some ways my sister and I were quite alike." I looked at him. "You had a sister. Certainly you and she were alike in some ways."

Except for the slight tightening of his jaw, I would have thought he hadn't heard my mention of Amelia.

"I don't mean in obvious ways like your appearance, your shared history as sisters, or as women in general," he retorted. "I mean in other ways."

"Other ways?"

"I loved your sister, Ophelia, and she loved me. We knew each other inside and out, and I don't see her in you at all."

"That's because I am not her, Mr. Devlin." I sounded positively waspish.

"You're a bitter little thing, aren't you?"

I stared at him in surprise. Bitter? No one had ever called me bitter. Yet something in the description resonated within me, and I looked away from his knowing gaze.

"Devlin, that was quite unkind," Nellie scolded. "You should apologize to Ophelia."

"No," he drawled, shaking his head. "I think she just might need to think on it, twirl it over in that busy little mind of hers—Desi always said that was her way—and determine the truth of it herself. After she's had some time to do that, I'll answer all the questions she has."

"How could you possibly know I have questions?"

"I doubt you wanted what your sister did when she

135

called on me."

I blushed at the innuendo in his words, and gathered my dignity about me like a cloak.

"I'm not calling on you," I said haughtily. "I'm calling on Nellie."

"You were on your way to see me."

"No, I wasn't. I—"

He laughed before I could finish forming the lie. "Donald Calhoun brought a message from his sister that you were on your way. She was concerned you'd break your foolish neck on the jetty rocks trying to find me. Probably afraid Cade would fire her for telling you where to look, too, but that wasn't in her message."

"That's where you were going?" Nellie gasped. "Thank goodness I stopped you. Those rocks are dangerously slick and sharp. Many a man's cut himself badly on those things."

"You won't tell him she told me, will you?" I asked him, ignoring Nellie's exclamation.

"My dear Ophelia, I won't tell and he won't listen, so Dory's little secret is safe between us."

"What do you think happened to my sister?" The question was out before I could stop it, and the next one was even more of a surprise. "Do you think Cade killed your sister, too?"

"I just told you I wasn't telling you a thing, even though your use of the word 'too' opens up a whole new can of worms. Bitterness can tint all one sees, even those you love."

"I am not bitter," I enunciated each word.

"Yes, you are. And until you accept it, you'll never forgive her." His voice softened, and he looked at me sadly. "Why couldn't you just forgive her, Ophelia?"

"Forgive Desi? For what?" Nellie asked, her natural curiosity taking over.

Devlin cocked one dark eyebrow at me. "It seems my little bird stole her sister's future. Now, the only way for Ophelia to get it back is to forgive the past."

I gasped. Was he saying he knew something that could keep Cade from hanging, and he wouldn't tell me until I forgave Desi? Would a posthumous pardon quiet the ghosts that haunted my nights? Suddenly desperate for both, I leapt to my feet.

"I forgive her!" I cried, leaning toward him. "I forgive her. Now, tell me how she died!"

"Liar!" he hissed. His eyes went cold, then hot, burning with hatred and something wild and frightening. He stood up slowly, his face pale except for two bright splotches of color high on his cheeks.

"Devlin, sit down. There's no need to get worked up," Nellie coaxed, as if she were talking to a mad dog.

He ignored her as his hand shot out and grabbed my wrist. Nellie cried out as he dragged me through the door.

I dug my feet into the ground, but it was no use. He overpowered me with every turn. Nellie followed behind us, begging him to stop, but he paid her no heed. His grasp on me only tightened, sending pain shooting through my wrist and up my arm.

"Devlin, please, stop, you can't do this." Nellie's hand grasped at his arm, but he shook her off. She was caught off balance and fell to her side with a cry.

"No!" I begged, trying to break free of him. "Nellie! Devlin, please stop! We have to help her!"

He lengthened his stride, and I slid down, landing on my backside and staying there. He dragged me several feet before bending down, and with a muttered curse, hefting me over his shoulder. Behind us, Nellie managed to get up from the ground and staggered toward the road that led to the village, her hand wrapped protectively around her bulging stomach.

We reached the lighthouse, and he pulled open the door. The staircase was dark, the air damp and dank, as he climbed higher and higher. I no longer fought him. Instead, I concentrated on making peace with the Lord. I had not expected to die so young or so violently. There was so much I had not done, so many dreams I had never realized. I prayed for forgiveness of my sins. I prayed for the few loved ones I would leave behind, Cade and Tabby, Mrs. Dupree and John Bailey. I prayed that I was ready to meet my Savior. And I was haunted by Devlin's voice, his biting assessment of me as a "bitter little thing." How long had bitterness held me in its grip? Since John Bailey handed me the letter announcing the marriage of my sister and Cade? Had it taken root at that moment? Or had that simply been the moment it blossomed after years of lying dormant? Had it taken root much earlier, perhaps the moment our mother breathed her last and one of us was chosen to take her place by our father's side? Had I always been envious of my sister's freedom to act as she desired instead of as society dictated?

Had Desdemona thought of these things as she made this journey? Had she regretted the past or had she faced death with satisfaction in her life?

It was ironic that we were to die the same death when we had lived such different lives.

When at last we reached the door that opened onto the upper deck, Devlin lowered me to my feet.

"You want to know what happened to your sister?" he growled. "Let me show you."

He pulled open the door, and pushed me out ahead of him. The wind whipped at my gown and hair, and I plastered myself to the wall, afraid to go near the edge. While I could well imagine Desi loving it here, being so high off solid ground turned my body to stone. If I went over the railing, it would be by sheer force, not my own folly.

"She came here all the time," Devlin said, digging in his pockets until he found what he sought, a bright red sash he worked through his hands as he spoke. He seemed to relax, perhaps because he realized my phobia would keep me from trying to escape. "She said she felt as if she shared the view with the birds alone. Both Cade and I warned her of the dangers, of the crumbling mortar and slickness of the stone when it was wet. But she came anyway, rain or shine. At least once a day, more if the urge struck her, she was here, dreaming of flying away."

He leaned against the wall beside me, once again calm, and speaking in those soft cultured tones he'd used in Nellie's presence.

"Was she so unhappy?" I panted, my heart thudding in my chest so hard I could hardly breathe.

"Yes."

The distant rumble of thunder reached us, and he looked toward the horizon.

"It had been raining for a week when she died."

"Cade said it was a clear day."

He ignored me and went on.

"She often grew melancholy when it rained. They said she left Almenara before the sun was even up. The

139

sunrise was purple that morning, and the clouds were so low they circled the top of the lighthouse. When I saw them, I knew she'd be here even though it had been raining all night and the stairs would be a hazard. She loved it when she could touch the clouds."

Was this a confession, I wondered. It hardly mattered, of course, as I wouldn't live to repeat it to anyone else.

"I found her, you know. She was broken and battered, a little swallow who fell from the sky, crushed upon the rocks." He took a shuddering breath, and closed his eyes against the memory. "I suppose our Amelia looked the same when Calvin found her there."

"Did you see what happened to my sister?" I forced the question out through the lump in my throat.

"Yes. Just as I saw what happened to mine." The word was a ragged whisper of pain, and it sent a shiver of fear up my spine.

With one violent shove, he turned me so that my stomach was pressed against the wall and my hands behind my back. Before I could think to fight, he had my hands bound and my eyes covered with the sash.

Terror came with sightlessness and my breath froze, coming in short shallow gasps that left me lightheaded and weak. I pressed my cheek against the cold hard stone, afraid to move lest I fall over the edge.

"Why are you doing this?"

"You are to Cade what she was to me, and I want him to feel the fear."

I shook my head in denial, and he pressed his mouth to my ear.

"He killed her, Ophelia. I watched him do it."

Chapter Sixteen

With those words, he was gone, and I was alone on the parapet, his words beating in my head like a drum with every panicked heartbeat. Relief that I was still alive washed over me, and I sank to my knees, my cheek running the length of the wall as I moved. I ignored the painful scraping of skin against stone and the jarring pain of my knees meeting the ground. I don't know how long I leaned there against the wall, my arms growing numb and my back throbbing, before the first fat raindrop hit me. Even through the blindfold, I could see the lightning streak across the sky, followed by a clap of thunder that seemed to shake the very foundation of the lighthouse. Still afraid to move away from the wall, I attempted to turn so that my back was pressed against it. I managed only to fall on my side, and with my hands tied behind my back, it was impossible to right myself.

I screamed until my voice was raw, hoping and praying Nellie had made it to the village and would soon send someone to help me. Realizing she could very well have been hurt herself, I tried to force my worry for myself away so that I could pray for her. In the end, I simply prayed fervently for us both as the deluge of rain beat against me with icy precision and my body shook with equal measures of terror and cold.

The rain ended as quickly as it had begun, and as

the skies quieted, I heard the sound of footsteps inside the lighthouse. My breath froze in my chest. Had he returned? Did he intend to kill me now?

The scraping of the door, followed by a vicious curse, and his hands were upon me, ripping the blindfold from my eyes. Cade appeared before me like an avenging angel, and I wondered wildly if this was the last visage my sister had looked upon. My mind spun with disbelief and fear, and with a whimper, I scooted away from him.

"No," he barked, his dark eyes boring into mine, denying the fear he saw there. "No."

I stopped my retreat, and he unbound my hands before pulling me against him.

"Inside," I said through chattering teeth. Tremors shook my body so hard I could barely speak. "Take me inside."

He muttered something my teeth were rattling too loudly for me to hear and lifted me in his arms. My fear dissipated into sudden relief, and I clung to him, my face buried against his neck. When I was close to him, it was impossible for me to consider him a murderer. When he pressed his lips against my hair, I was able to silence the small voice that reminded me that all the facts pointed to him, whether I chose to consider it or not.

Once we were inside the relative safety of the lighthouse, he stopped and leaned against the door. His breath was ragged against my hair as he continued to hold me.

"My God, Fee, I was terrified I'd find you on the rocks below." His voice broke, and I lifted my head to peer at him through the dim light. "Did he hurt you?"

"No." I nestled even closer against him, letting the warmth of his body seep into mine.

He let out a shuddering breath. "Thank God. Thank God."

The hardness and heat of him emanated through his clothes and mine, and a sudden, desperate hunger consumed me. The moment our lips met, I knew I was lost. I was no longer the innocent young girl I had been that long-ago season, nor was I the innocent, levelheaded spinster I had been mere days ago. I was a woman who wanted this man, despite the very real possibility that he had murdered my sister and another woman, and despite the violence I sensed in him. None of that mattered to me. All I wanted was to be with him, to know him as I'd never known another man, with a passion I had never dreamed existed inside of me.

He was the one to break the kiss, and his name was a plea on my lips.

"They'll be looking for us, Fee. The cry went up and the men will be here any moment to make sure you are safe."

As if on cue, I heard the other men downstairs.

"Cade!" Calvin bellowed from the bottom of the winding staircase. "Have you found her?"

"She's here! I'm bringing her down now."

Calvin, Dennis, and James Arnold waited for us at the ground level. At the sight of James, shame flooded through me. The last time I'd seen his very pregnant wife, she'd been dragging herself up from the ground, intent on getting help for me. Her welfare should have been my first concern, and because of my own indecent desire for Cade Scott, I hadn't given her a thought once I'd seen him.

"Was Nellie hurt?" I asked him now.

"No, she's fine, other than being out of her head with worry. She'll be right as rain once we get you safely home."

"Any sign of Devlin?" Cade's eyes searched the shore and the tree line beyond.

"No, but I've got men searching the woods," Calvin answered. To me, he said, "Well, Miss Garrett, I guess you're no smarter than your sister was, going off on your own without telling a soul. It's a miracle you didn't come to the same end she did."

It was on the tip of my tongue to tell him I had told someone, but I didn't want to get Dory in trouble, so I lied instead. "I only intended a short walk. I never dreamed I'd be in danger."

I ignored Cade's sound of disbelief as he tightened his grip on me and pushed past the other men. I had little doubt he knew exactly what had led me to Nellie's gate.

Cade deposited me just inside Nellie's front door with a stern warning to stay inside. Although I cringed at his commanding tone, I acquiesced with a slight nod of my head and turned my attention to Nellie, who lay back on the sofa, a damp rag on her head and the doctor bending over her solicitously.

"Oh, Nellie, are you all right?" I gasped, rushing toward her.

"I'm fine, Fee. The fall was just a little jarring, and James wouldn't rest until the doctor had checked me."

"Of course not. It's always better to be safe than sorry."

I looked toward Richard for confirmation that she was fine, and he nodded as he snapped his bag shut. He looked nearly as murderous as Cade had when he appeared on the parapet, and warmth rushed to my face. My disobedience of his orders had caused quite an uproar, and I realized now that my actions could have caused horrible repercussions for others as well as myself. How would I have lived with myself if Nellie or her baby had been injured?

"You look like hell," Richard said curtly, causing Nellie to protest his rudeness from her place on the sofa.

"Don't admonish him, Nellie. I'm fairly certain he's right."

She lifted the rag from her head and peered at me. "Oh, heavens, Fee, you're soaked through. Go into my room and grab one of the dresses from my closet. Those in the front are all for my pregnancy, so you'll want one from the back. You'll find undergarments in the top drawer of the bureau. Use whatever you need."

I protested that I would dry and be fine, but when she made to get up to find me something suitable to wear, I urged her to lie back down and hurried to do as she bid.

I reached to the back of the closet and pulled out the first dress my hand met. I had rather hoped her overabundance of ruffles and flounces was a temporary proclivity used to divert attention from her rounded belly. Judging from the ruffled, canary yellow confection I held in my hand, I was wrong. I refused to rifle through her closet in a futile attempt to find a more suitable dress. I would only have to wear it on the ride back to Almenara, after all, and it was doubtful anyone but Cade and Nellie would see me. I pulled open the bureau drawer she had indicated, but pushed it shut without removing anything.

I doubted there was a vicar's wife in the country whose undergarments were so embellished, but then, I had already guessed that Nellie Arnold was one of a kind. With a sigh, I slipped out of my wet dress and dropped the yellow mass of ruffles and bows over my head. My own undergarments were of plain white linen and would dry quickly enough. I much preferred to wear them under a dry dress than to borrow the lace-and-bow-adorned things Nellie favored.

I pulled the two remaining pins from my hair and ran the brush through it. I watched in the mirror as it sprang back into wet black waves, which I tried to secure to my head in some respectable fashion. As I viewed my reflection, I decided that a few loose locks of hair were the least of my worries. Although Nellie was an inch or so taller than I and even outside of pregnancy quite a bit wider in the hips and waist, her bosom was considerably smaller than mine. So although the dress had ample room in the skirt, the ruffled bosom pulled tightly against my breasts, which seemed close to spilling from the top.

I let my hair down, arranging it about my shoulders so it covered the exposed skin above the neckline of the dress, or at least a portion of skin.

Not for the first time, I wondered how Nellie had come to be the wife of the quiet and reserved Reverend Arnold.

I breathed a sigh of relief as I came out of the bedroom. No one but Nellie was present in the house. Richard's bag still rested on the chair where he'd left it, so I assumed he had joined the men in the hunt for Devlin. I sincerely hoped they would all stay gone until

146

I was safely in the carriage heading back to Almenara.

"Come," she said, patting the stool beside her. "Tell me what happened after Devlin took you away."

"You don't seem surprised that I'm uninjured," I observed as I sat and arranged the ruffled skirt around me as best I could.

"Of course I'm not surprised. I never thought Devlin would injure you."

"Why did you try to stop him?"

"You were terrified, and he was being unreasonable. I was afraid that was a sure recipe for disaster."

"How well do you know him?"

She sighed, and pulled the cloth from her head. "Well enough to know he wouldn't hurt you on purpose, but could very well let his proclivity for rashness cause you injury."

"Proclivity for rashness?" I repeated the phrase, surprised at her tactful description of what others might consider utter insanity.

"Yes, like knocking me down. Devlin in his right mind would never do such a thing, but when worked up, he hardly even noticed he'd done it."

"I'm not sure that is better than knowingly doing it."

"Well, I'm sure it is," she said. "Intent is what creates malice. And I'm right. Once he calmed down, he didn't injure you, did he?"

"He bound my hands, blindfolded me, and left me outside on the parapet at the top of the lighthouse. I was trapped in the storm. It was terrifying."

"But you weren't injured, except for the scrapes on your face," she observed sharply. "Wet and cold, but

147

not gravely injured."

"No, not gravely injured," I agreed, wondering at her continued defense of the man. Had I been able to stand, I could easily have tumbled over the side. He may not have intended for me to die, but I wasn't so sure he had intended me to live, either.

A loud crack of thunder sounded through the house and she jumped. Then, with her usual trifling laugh, she looked at me apologetically. "I apologize if I sound as if I'm excusing his actions, Fee. I'm certain you were scared out of your wits up there. I'm safely inside and the sound of another storm makes me tremble."

A second rumble of thunder, and Richard dashed back inside, closing his umbrella as he entered.

"The sky let loose again as soon as I got to the cemetery. I expect the others will be back any minute." Seeing me sitting beside Nellie, he came to me.

"Let me look at you, Ophelia." He took my chin in his hand and turned my face to study the scraped and bleeding skin on my cheek. "How did this happen?"

"I scraped it against the stone." My voice broke and tears pooled in my eyes. Given Nellie's dismissal of my ordeal, I was ashamed at how raw my emotions were, and I tried to smile as I assured him I was fine.

His eyes softened and, without a word, he wrapped his arms around me and pulled me against him gently.

I let him hold me, wishing I could feel for him what I felt for Cade. How much simpler my life would be if I could, but it was impossible. I would never feel for another man what I felt for Cade, and I would rather live alone for the rest of my life than live with a man for whom I didn't feel that soul-stirring passion. I wondered if I would someday regret not settling for a good man who could love me and whom I could learn to love in turn. Why could I not find contentment in the gentle sort of love that would afford me children and a loving companion as I grew old?

The door opened, and I pulled away from Richard's hold as the other men poured in.

"Did you find him?" Nellie asked her husband.

"No, and the storm's come back around, so we aren't going to look anymore tonight."

Cade and Dennis Ames were the last to enter and, although deep in conversation, Cade shot a glance my way as they entered. I had no doubt the frightful picture I made, encompassed by overwrought ruffles and unbound hair, but I was still surprised at his reaction. His eyes widened and he stopped in mid-sentence. Dennis also stared at me, his face a fiery red, and I self-consciously smoothed my hair over my shoulders.

"If you're up to it, I think we can beat the storm home," Cade said gruffly. His eyes shot to Richard, who still stood in close enough proximity to touch me, before returning to my over-exposed bosom.

"Yes, please," I said, aware that all eyes were now upon me. I had never thought of myself as vain, so I was surprised at how unnerved I was by my disheveled and possibly comical condition. I gathered up my own wet dress and turned to Nellie. "Thank you for loaning me your dress. I'll have it cleaned and returned to you."

Cade draped his coat over my shoulders, murmuring something about a chill, and we dashed into the windswept yard.

Once we were settled inside the carriage, he turned toward me, a smile curving his handsome mouth. "What in the devil are you wearing?"

"A dress." I could barely suppress my laughter.

"I don't know if I would call that mess below the waist a dress, and the tiny bit of material at the top most definitely does not qualify." His eyes rested on the display of cleavage afforded by the bodice, and I felt my face redden. He lifted his face to mine and studied me for a moment, his eyes dark with desire. "You still blush like you did when you were a girl."

I pursed my lips, embarrassed by my lack of experience. "I've never learned to control it."

"I sincerely hope you never do." He stroked the hair curling about my shoulders. "It is quite becoming."

"I am a confirmed spinster, Cade. I should have learned the art of self-control long ago."

"I can't get my mind around the thought of you as a spinster, Fee."

"You must accept it. I have." I cringed at how easily the lie slid from my lips.

"Why didn't you ever marry?" His fingers brushed the skin of my throat and a shiver raced up my spine as my eyes slid closed.

"I had to care for my father." It was the reason I had given for the last six years, but Cade chuckled softly. Of course, he recognized my lie and the purr of desire that tinged my voice.

His fingers continued their gentle, swirling exploration of my hair and throat, and I fought the urge to lean my head back, exposing the sensual curve of my throat to his hands and lips.

"Your father has been gone enough years, Ophelia. Surely you could have married since then, if not before. You certainly must have had suitors. You've been at Almenara only a week and you already have our stoic

Dr. Scarborough acting like a besotted schoolboy."

My eyes flew open, and I met his dark gaze. Was he toying with me? Did he want me to admit that my memories of him had kept me in their grip all these years, or to tell of the futile dreams I had dreamed as I lay alone in my childhood bed, knowing my sister lay in his? I wanted to demand he acknowledge that he knew why I was still alone, but instead I shrugged and spoke the truth for him to read into it what he would.

"I could never marry without love."

Chapter Seventeen

It began to rain again as we pulled to a stop in front of Almenara, and Cade grabbed my hand as we rushed up the stone steps. The feel of his warm hand on mine brought back a rush of memories.

We had once taken a hackney to the New Orleans riverfront to watch the barges being unloaded. Unwilling to have the afternoon end with a quick ride back to the hotel, we decided to walk the distance. We ignored the darkening skies and distant thunder, and began our trek back hand in hand. Halfway there, the sky opened up and rain poured down upon us. We laughed and ran, as only the young will do, ignoring the grim warnings of the few old men we passed. Within moments, the wind picked up and the first hail rained down. I screeched when the icy pellets hit me, and Cade scooped me up over his shoulder. Both of us were still laughing as he hurried toward the one open door along the sidewalk.

The warehouse was dark and empty and smelled of the sea, but I hardly noticed any of that as Cade let me down. I slid down his body, feeling his desire match my own. He buried his hands in my hair, and lowered his mouth to mine. Our kisses there in the cool, unlit interior of the warehouse were far different from the ones we had shared before, which while not exactly chaste, had not been as passionate as those we shared in the salted darkness around us. I have never doubted that had a group of oystermen not chosen that moment to enter the warehouse, Cade and I would have consummated our love within its darkened depths.

As it was, we broke apart, waited out the storm with the others, and hurried to the hotel. It was upon our return to the hotel that Mrs. Dupree handed me the letter that would put Cade and Desi's betrayal in motion. My sister would arrive by train two days later. Little did I know as I read her message that I would leave New Orleans and my dreams of the future behind shortly after her arrival.

Now, I stood on the porch of Almenara, a twenty-five-year-old virgin, my hand in Cade's and the same girlish longings beating in my chest.

I pulled my hand away and dashed ahead of him, nearly colliding with Eleanor, who was pacing the foyer in agitation, her face pale and her eyes red-rimmed from weeping.

"Ophelia!" she cried when she saw me. "Are you well?"

"Yes," I murmured, trying to push past her. She placed a hand on my arm, and I stopped.

"And Devlin?" Her voice was barely above a whisper, but I heard the devastating worry in her voice. I realized then what I should have known all along. Eleanor was madly and inexplicably in love with Devlin.

"He's fine," Cade assured her. "The men looked for him, but they couldn't find him. Nellie is pleading for them to let him alone, and I feel certain she'll get her way. By tomorrow, it should all have blown over."

Eleanor looked so relieved I feared she might faint,

while I stared at him in surprise. It would all have blown over? As if what Devlin did to me was nothing? As if what Devlin said had been nothing? Was that why Cade could act so calm? Because he knew Devlin hadn't intended to kill me? Was he so certain Devlin wasn't a murderer—because *he* was?

Over his cousin's head, our eyes met, and I wondered if the questions in his gaze were directed toward Eleanor's distress or mine.

When Eleanor walked toward the stairs, I followed her, intent on getting away from Cade. I could not forget the way he had run his fingers through my hair, the way he had spoken to me in the carriage. I was the only one who had been certain of his innocence. What would he do to keep me on his side? Would he seduce me? Did he expect me to become so blinded by him that I overlooked the accusations, the evidence, and the opinion of every single person around us?

"Fee."

I was halfway up the stairs when I heard him say my name, and I turned to him, silently commanding myself to ignore the injured tone.

He spoke so softly I barely heard him. "You aren't the only one who remembers New Orleans."

It was tempting to believe we could build a future on those memories, but I knew it was only a pretty lie. Whether it was intentional or not, those memories and every day between them and now was nothing but blood-soaked sand beneath our feet.

"It doesn't really matter now, does it, Cade?" I asked. "Those days are long gone."

I didn't wait for his reply before hurrying up the stairs, nearly colliding with Eleanor and Lorraine, who both stood there just beyond the landing. I ignored Lorraine's rather smug smile as well as Eleanor's continued cries for Devlin's safety. I wasn't in any mood to speak with either of them, and was quite frightened I might take my frustration out on Eleanor if I had to listen to her natter on for one more moment.

"I hear you had quite the exciting day," Lorraine said as I passed.

"Yes, quite," I agreed without stopping.

"What on earth are you wearing?"

I looked down at the yellow dress. "My clothes were wet, so I borrowed Nellie's dress."

"I should have known. I sometimes wonder if Reverend Arnold didn't find that silly chit in a brothel."

I opened my mouth, intending to tell her exactly what I thought about her insults toward Nellie, but decided it would do no good and clamped my mouth shut.

"Eleanor, perhaps you should rest," I suggested. "I'm sure Cade will let you know if there's any word of Devlin."

"Cade will kill him if he finds him. He's already said so," she sobbed. "He was crazed with worry when he heard Devlin took you. Even Nellie couldn't calm him."

"Well, he can see for himself I'm fine. There's no need for him to retaliate. Devlin did me no real harm. Like Cade said, by tomorrow it will all have blown over."

"Devlin is quite mad," Lorraine said, and lifted a hand to stop Eleanor's protest. "I'm surprised he didn't toss you over the railing of the lighthouse."

I said nothing and she went on.

"I guess he isn't quite as mad as Cade. As far as I know, Devlin's never murdered anyone."

"As far as I know, Cade hasn't either," I argued.

Her mouth curved into the smile I was coming to know.

"He's been arrested for murder, Ophelia dear. And within the month, he'll hang for it. No matter your feelings toward him, even you can't be so blind to the writing on the wall."

My stomach roiled at the similarities between her words and my own suspicions.

"Cade couldn't have killed Desdemona," I protested, but it sounded weak even to my own ears.

"Someone killed her. And as my husband has told you, Cade is the only person with any real motive at all." She cocked one eyebrow, and I could imagine how convincing she'd been on stage. "At least that's what everyone thought until now."

"What does that mean?" But I knew what it meant. It meant she had noticed the attraction between Cade and me. It meant I could be a suspect in Desdemona's death because, God help me, I was as in love with Cade today as I had always been.

"You know what it means, Ophelia."

My temper flared, but I controlled the urge to slap the mocking smile off her face, straightened my spine and met her eyes.

"You're right, Lorraine. It has been a very exciting day, and I find I am utterly exhausted. I think I'll rest a while before supper."

With that, I walked sedately to my room, my head held high until the door closed behind me. At the sound of the soft thud, the events of the day crashed down upon me, and I felt so dizzy and ill that I could hardly stand. I removed my dress, staggered to the bed, and rolled the quilt around me like a cocoon.

I didn't wake until Dory came in to help me dress for dinner. My head was pounding, my appetite was nonexistent, and I was sorely tempted to make my excuses and skip dinner. I refused to give Lorraine that satisfaction, however, and instead had Dory do my hair in a much more elaborate style than normal. I pulled the dress of midnight blue silk from the wardrobe and let Dory help me slip it over my head. I prayed that tonight would not end with my fleeing the room as I had the last time I'd worn it. At least now I understood Cade's anger, even if I was shocked that he thought me so devious that I would trick him into marrying Desi because she was pregnant.

"Are you sure you're okay, miss?" Dory asked, peering over my shoulder at my reflection in the dressing table mirror. "You look a bit peaked."

"I'm fine, Dory." She was right, of course. I was quite pale and wan.

I had never been one for lip rouge and face paint, but my sister had always adored both, so I excused myself as soon as I was dressed and went to the room I knew had been hers.

Her dressing table was a mess, as I had expected it to be, and a wave of relief washed over me as I looked around. Several dresses were cast carelessly about, a haphazard stack of books leaned against the table by her bed, and a pair of shoes lay by the open wardrobe as if she had just stepped out of them. It was good to see that at least something about Desi had remained unchanged until the end. Nostalgia clung to me as I sank onto the small upholstered stool and rummaged through the clutter on the dressing table. I applied bright lip rouge to my mouth and imagined Desi sitting here, primping and posturing as she readied for the day ahead. The day she died.

I stared deep into the mirror, as if I could somehow see her there in my own reflection. Had she known the last time she'd sat here that it would be the final day of her life? Had there been any warning that someone wanted her dead? She had obviously dressed with care that day, casting aside her choices until she found the dress she ultimately wore. What had she worn the day she died? I wondered if she had intended to meet Devlin, if that was why she left the house early. Who had decided she would never step foot in this room again? And why?

Looking down at the dressing table, I reached for a monogrammed handkerchief that covered a small, soft-looking mound. I lifted it, expecting to find a wayward glove or stocking, and, if I was lucky, a bit of perfume.

A scream erupted from my throat and I pulled back quickly at the sight of the decomposing body of the barn swallow lying on the dresser, a porcelain hat pin thrust through its tiny chest.

"What the devil?" Cade was at my side in an instant, followed by Dory and Mrs. Hartley. I pointed to the bird, and he swore under his breath. "Mrs. Hartley, have someone remove the remains of that poor creature immediately."

He gripped my elbow and hauled me from the room.

"What were you doing in her room?"

"I was looking for lip rouge," I said, stammering

when he scowled down at me. "I don't have any, and I knew Desi would."

"I don't recall you wearing lip rouge."

"I felt a bit peaked tonight. I thought it might help."

Concern darkened his gaze and he took my chin in his hand, studying me closely. "Of course you feel peaked after the day you had. Still, I'll send for the doctor."

"No. I'm fine. It's only my appearance that is a bit worse for the wear. We shouldn't interrupt Richard's supper for something as trivial as a bit of feminine vanity."

"But you could be ill, and I'm certain he wouldn't mind the interruption."

I shrugged. "It's more likely that I have a bit of a chill from being caught in the rain. Let's wait and see. If I'm still out of sorts in the morning, you can send for him."

"Very well," he said after a second or two of consideration. "Are you ready to go down to supper now?"

I glanced down at the handkerchief in my hand. I was somehow able to keep my surprise silent as I realized that someone had written something on it. There was no time to read it now, not with Cade waiting to escort me to dinner, but I had a feeling it was important that I know what it said. Afraid I would misplace it or it would be noticed by someone at dinner, I lifted my face to Cade.

"I am feeling a bit chilled and would like to retrieve my shawl first."

His eyes narrowed, and I knew he was considering

whether he should go against my wishes and call for Richard. Before he could command that I go to bed and await the doctor's arrival, I hurried to my room. When I realized he had followed me, I pulled my shawl from the back of the chair by the fireplace. My book lay open on the table, and I deftly slipped the handkerchief between the pages before snapping it shut and turning back to Cade.

He leaned against the doorjamb, his feet crossed at the ankles, hands in his pockets. In that moment, the weary resolve seemed to have fallen away and he looked achingly young. Tears welled in my eyes, and I dashed them away. It was no use crying over what could not be changed.

He straightened as I walked toward him, and when I was close enough, he reached out and ran a gentle hand over my cheek to cup my jaw.

"Are you sure you feel like going down, Fee? No one would blame you if you didn't."

Lorraine's tinkling laughter wafted down the hall, and I silently gathered myself.

"I'm fine," I lied as I placed my hand in the crook of his arm. The fingers I wrapped around his warm bicep were the only part of me that wasn't chilled to the bone.

I glanced into the framed mirror at the head of the stairs as we passed. No wonder Cade wanted to call the doctor. I wasn't sure if my unnatural pallor was due to my earlier ordeal, an oncoming illness, or the garish red paint on my lips combined with the large raw spot where my cheek had scraped against the lighthouse wall. I nearly stopped and fled back to the sanctuary of my bedroom, but I heard Lorraine and Calvin talking behind us, and I had no choice but to proceed to the dining room if I didn't wish to make a scene.

By the end of supper, I knew I was ill. My head swam, and I could feel the heat of my cheeks on my hand. My limbs felt weighted, and it was an effort to follow the conversation around me. When dessert was finally served, I placed my napkin on the table.

"If you all will excuse me, I think I will retire for the night."

"You look positively ill," Lorraine remarked.

"I really don't feel very well," I informed her, pushing myself to my feet.

I barely made it to the end of the table before my legs seemed to give way beneath me. I put a hand on the table and steadied myself.

I heard Cade's chair scraped back from the table, and I shook my head. "I'm fine, Cade. You've hefted me around enough for one day. I'll see you in the morning."

I was able to exit the room with some dignity intact and pulled myself up the stairs, clinging to the banister. I was halfway up when I felt Cade's strong arms sweep me off my feet. I hadn't the strength to even cling to his neck as he carried me to the bedroom and pulled the bell pull. Laying me on the bed, he removed my shoes and stockings.

My protests were feeble at best, and I was as limp as a dishrag as he maneuvered me around, trying to unbutton my dress.

"Yes, miss?" Dory said brightly as she came in. A small gasp of surprise followed her greeting, and she hurried to the bed, shooing Cade away. "Get her a nightgown, Mr. Cade."

I drifted in and out of wakefulness as Cade moved to the bureau and Dory instructed him on where to find a gown. Then he was back again, pulling me upright, his strong, warm arm encircling my waist.

"Let me hold her while you get this blasted dress off her," he told Dory.

"I can call for Mrs. Hartley or one of the other—" Her protest seemed to die on her lips, and I could well imagine the look he gave her to quell it.

A chill swept through me, and I shivered violently in his arms. He murmured some soft nonsense and pressed his lips to the top of my aching head. By the time they had me undressed, gowned and tucked in bed, I was racked by chills and my teeth chattered in my head.

"She's burning with fever, Mr. Cade."

"Calvin's gone for the doctor."

"Poor miss. It's the rain did it to her. That daft man shouldn't have left her up there like that."

Even through the clouds in my head, I heard the murderous rage in Cade's low voice. "He'll be sorry he ever touched her."

Chapter Eighteen

It took extreme determination to open my eyes to the bright sunshine streaming through the windows of my room. On the first try, I moaned and snapped my eyelids shut against it, but the second attempt was a success and, very slowly, the room came into focus. Cade stood in front of the largest window, silhouetted by the sun as he stared at some distant point beyond the garden. He must have heard my futile efforts to sit up, because he turned toward the bed, looking exhausted and haggard with worry.

"Fee," he choked, gathering me against him. He took several long breaths, as if trying to get hold of himself. "Thank God, you're awake. We were afraid you wouldn't make it another night."

"How long have I been ill?"

"Your fever raged for four nights. It finally broke earlier this morning."

Four nights? I had always prided myself on my hearty constitution, and the thought of being brought so low by being out in the rain was hard for me to accept.

"I've been rained on before, Cade, and I've never gotten anything more than a bit of a chill."

"Richard says you were already in a weakened state from the trauma of Desi's death and your fall at the lighthouse. When Devlin accosted you and left you in the storm, your body wasn't able to fight illness off as it normally might."

I shuddered at the reminder of those sightless, terrifying moments at the top of the lighthouse. I could almost feel Devlin's breath on my neck as he whispered those horrible words.

He killed her, Ophelia. I watched him do it.

"What is it? You've gone white as a sheet." He placed a hand on my head, feeling for fever. "Perhaps you should lie back down."

"I'm fine," I assured him. "Just lingering effects of the fever, I daresay."

"I've brought the breakfast you've asked for, sir," Dory said quietly from the doorway. Her brow was drawn together with worry, but upon seeing me awake, a wide smile stretched across her pretty face. "Oh, miss, praise be! You're awake!"

She set Cade's tray on the table in front of the windows and then turned to me.

"I've brought eggs and ham for Mr. Cade. Would you like me to fetch you some? Or Cook makes porridge for Miss Tabby every morning. Perhaps, you'd prefer that."

"Thank you, Dory, but I'm really not hungry." At her look of dismay and worry, however, I offered a smile and nodded. "Actually, a nice bowl of hot porridge would be lovely. With a bit of honey and butter, if it's no bother."

"Oh, no, miss. It's no bother at all. I'll bring it right up. And a pot of tea, as well."

She darted from the room, and I closed my eyes for a moment. I had never felt so weak in my life.

"You are not feeling well enough to worry about hurt feelings, Ophelia," Cade groused from the table.

"I wasn't worrying about her feelings."

"You claimed not to be hungry, and then I assume she looked crestfallen, so you changed your mind. Now you'll feel obligated to eat all of your porridge out of some misguided notion of politeness."

My stomach chose that very opportune moment to rumble loudly, and I gave him a triumphant smile.

He shook his head and began eating his breakfast.

The upholstered chair that usually faced the fireplace had been pulled to the side of my bed, and I wondered if he'd been here the entire time I was ill. His face was gray with exhaustion, and a scraggly beard shadowed his chin. As I watched, his head nodded over his breakfast.

"You're exhausted, Cade. Why don't you go to your room and rest?"

He scrubbed a hand over his face and shook his head.

"No, I'm fine. I'll stay with you until Richard arrives."

"At least go and bathe, Cade. Richard won't come and go while you refresh yourself."

"I'll wait for Dory to return."

"No, you won't. I want to bathe and rest, and I can't do either with you here. Go."

"Do you swear you'll stay put? You won't go traipsing off to parts unknown as soon as I leave the room?"

"I swear I've learned my lesson, Cade. Besides, I don't think I could possibly get very far."

"No, I suppose you couldn't." He bent and kissed the top of my head. "I'll send Dory up to help you bathe."

Before he left, he went to the lavatory and turned the knobs on the tub.

"Wait for Dory. I don't want you falling over while you try to bathe."

When he was gone, I forced myself to stand, fighting my weakness and managing through sheer force of will to keep myself upright. With a huge effort, I was already soaking in the tub when Dory arrived with my breakfast tray.

She clucked disapprovingly but went to work changing my bed linens and laying out a clean nightgown as I bathed.

"It's good to see you on the mend, miss. We were all worried about you, but Mr. Cade was near crazed with it. He wouldn't leave your side. He just sat there holding your hand and talking to you real soft. I don't know what he said, but it seemed like the sound of his voice calmed you and you rested better."

"Dory, you weren't in trouble after my escapade, were you?"

"Of course not, miss," she said, but her voice was clipped, and I suspected she may have endured a setting down by someone. Whether it was Mrs. Hartley or Cade, I wasn't sure.

"If you were, I sincerely hope you'll forgive me. I should never have gotten you involved."

"I guessed you were lying when you said you weren't going to the cabin. If Miss Desi had been my sister, I'd have done the same. That's why I sent Donald ahead to warn Devlin. I hoped that man would meet you somewhere along the way. He isn't a safe man, miss, and he could have killed you easy enough. If you didn't break your neck crossing those rocks looking for him, that is."

"Could you do me another favor?" I asked, not missing the wariness in her eyes.

"I don't know, miss. I can't lie to Mr. Cade again, if that's what you're going to ask me to do."

"No, it was wrong of me to expect that of you, and what I want now is simply to have a message delivered."

"To who?"

"Nellie Arnold. I'd like to talk to her, and I would need her to come here, as I don't think Cade would let me go there."

"Mrs. Arnold couldn't possibly make it here, miss. She's already tried to start having the baby. The doctor put her to bed and told her to stay there, hoping to hold it off a little longer. But from what my mother said, it will most likely be any day now. Reverend Arnold's fit to be tied."

I knew that a fall like the one Nellie had taken when trying to stop Devlin could very well have caused her to go into premature labor. I'd been at my father's side several times when he was called to console women who lost their babies after giving birth early. Even with only a month before her due date, it was still dangerous for Nellie and the baby, and guilt overwhelmed me. How would I ever forgive myself if my recklessness caused either of them injury?

"I must go to her at once," I said, grabbing the towel and surging to my feet. My head spun from the sudden motion, but I fought off the lightheadedness and stepped out of the tub. "Get my gray plaid dress from the wardrobe, Dory."

The girl shook her head. "Mr. Cade gave strict

orders that you were to get back in bed as soon as your bath was over. I won't disobey him again, Miss Fee."

I moved past her and pulled the dress from my closet. "I'm not so helpless that I can't get dressed on my own, Dory. And if I do it on my own, then no one can blame you for it."

By the time I had the dress over my head, my room was empty, and I didn't have to think very hard to know where she'd gone. I was pulling on my stockings, sweat beading my brow from exertion, when my door flew open so hard it cracked against the wall.

"You little fool," Cade ground out as he marched toward me.

"Why didn't you tell me about Nellie?"

"You've been conscious for less than two hours, Ophelia. You nearly died. Forgive me if your health and wellbeing were foremost on my mind."

"Well, I'm fine now, and I must see about Nellie."

"You are not fine, and you are most certainly not leaving this house."

"I will do as I please, Cade, and you can't stop me." I glared at him. "You are my brother-in-law. You have no say over what I do."

"I'm a damn sight more than your brother-in-law, and we both know it."

He plucked my shoes from my grasp, and flung them at the wardrobe. He grabbed the bottle of medicine and poured a hefty dose into the spoon from the bedside table.

"Drink it," he ordered, holding it out to me.

"No."

"Ophelia, the doctor has ordered you to rest, and if you have to be drugged to do so, then by God, I'll drug you. You will take this medicine."

When I still refused, he used one arm to pin me against the mattress, as he tried to force the medicine through my pursed lips. Sobbing with frustration and still refusing to open my mouth, I put up a futile fight against him. Just when I felt as if my chest would burst from trying to breathe through my nose and fight against the pressure of his arm on my chest, I managed to jerk my head to the side hard enough to send the spoon flying from his hand.

I had never seen him so furious, and fear caught up what was left of the breath in my chest.

He killed her, Ophelia. I watched him do it. Had this terrifying fury been the last thing my sister had seen? Had he held her down as he tied her up? Had she known it was him who threw her to her death?

Suddenly afraid he might pour the whole bottle down my throat if I continued to fight him, I ceased my struggling.

"Please, Cade," I begged, my voice dry with fear. "I'll do as you say. Please, just let me go."

The fury in his eyes was replaced by startled surprise, and he stepped back, his eyes swinging from the open medicine bottle to me. I shot upright, gasping for air as I wondered if fear really could choke a body to death.

With a wounded cry, Cade hurled the bottle of laudanum across the room, where it crashed against the hearth in a puddle of shattered glass and liquid.

He reached for me, his arms falling to his sides when I moved away from him. "I would never hurt you, Fee."

"I don't believe you anymore," I whispered.

I wanted to believe him. I truly did. He looked old and tired and wounded, and I wanted to soothe the worry from his eyes and accept him at his word. Now that I had experienced his fury firsthand, however, doubt overcame me. Still, I needed to know Nellie was all right.

"I need to see Nellie. She might need my help."

"She's fine. Her sister is with her, and some of the ladies from the village."

"I've attended women during their lying-in before."

"You aren't attending anyone, Fee. Get that through your head. You are homebound for the next few days."

"This isn't my home."

My words silenced him, and he stood from the side of the bed, pacing back and forth while raking his hand through his hair. Finally, he stopped and came back to sit beside me. His dark eyes were nearly black with pain, and he took my hand in his. I controlled the desire to jerk it away from him.

"I know this isn't your home, and I'm sure you're more than ready to leave this godforsaken place, but I'm begging you to stay. I need you here. Just through the trial. I need to know that you will be here for Tabitha."

"I have no intention of leaving before the end of the trial, and there won't be any need for someone to look after Tabitha. You'll be here for her."

Tears welled in his eyes, and he looked away. "I know I can be harsh, and I can't seem to keep my distance from you. But you are the only person who has believed in me in a very long time. You make me remember the man I should be instead of the one I've become. I'm begging you not to stop."

"I'll be here." I couldn't promise I wouldn't stop believing in his innocence. Although I longed to feel as certain as I had the day I came to Almenara, I no longer was. It would do no good to lie to him or myself.

"You only have to rest a few more days, Ophelia. You aren't strong enough yet to be of any help to Nellie or anyone else."

"I know," I admitted. Then with a heavy heart, I looked him in the eye. "I'll agree to stay in bed until I'm stronger, Cade, but I need you to stay away from me."

"Of course," he agreed, and with a derisive bow that reeked of despair, he left the room.

****

Richard stopped by in the evening, and I questioned him thoroughly about Nellie as he checked my eyes and ears and listened to my heart. He ran his fingers beneath my chin, a small smile playing about his mouth as he did so.

"Cade tells me you've already tried to escape," he teased.

"I only wanted to check on Nellie. It wasn't as if I was going to traipse off into the wild."

His voice and eyes were stern when he spoke again.

"Obviously, you don't appreciate how ill you were, Ophelia. I believe you are out of the woods at this point, but you are far from well. Your lungs are still congested, and you are to rest until I say different. No more running about trying to solve crimes or catch ghosts. Do you understand?"

I grimaced. Had Cade actually told him about my ghostly visions? He laughed out loud.

"Calm yourself, sweetheart. Cade was concerned that your ghost sighting was a reaction to the medication, so he questioned me about it."

I tried to smile and laugh it off, but it bothered me immensely that the two of them had discussed me when I was not present. I was becoming increasingly ill-tempered, and Richard's next words set my teeth on edge.

"I don't know what is or was between you and Cade, Ophelia, but I can tell you that he cares deeply for you."

"He is my brother-in-law, Richard." I tried to sound appropriately offended by his implications.

He looked at me for a long moment, before his face brightened. "He was the boy you loved in New Orleans, wasn't he?"

"Yes," I admitted quietly.

"He didn't die. He married your sister."

"I never said he died. I only said he was gone."

"And you let Nellie infer that he died."

"Yes. I couldn't very well tell everyone the truth."

"So you aren't pining away for a dead lover?"

"No."

"Good," he said, his eyes gleaming with excitement. "Then I shall court you as if my competition for your affections is someone I can actually overcome, instead of a man upon whom sainthood has already been bestowed."

He snapped his bag shut, and with a bow much like Cade had left me with earlier, he was gone.

Chapter Nineteen

Richard's assurances that Nellie was in good hands eased my mind to the point that I was able to relax, and I slept soundly for the next night and most of the following day.

On Saturday, I woke at dawn feeling greatly renewed and sat at the table by the window. The rising sun dappled the water in the small fish pond below, and a family of cottontails hopped about in the grass between the garden and the woods.

For the first time since the night I fell ill, I thought of what I'd found in Desi's room. The poor dead bird, obviously killed with the blood-streaked hatpin in its chest, and the handkerchief, stained with several tiny droplets of blood and stark black ink.

With shaking hands, I reached for the book on the table. I pulled out the square of white linen, my fingers brushing across the dark blue embroidery thread that formed the letter at the corner. I turned it over, so that the finely lettered quote faced me, and I read it silently, each word cinching more tightly around my heart than the one before.

For murder, though it have no tongue,
will speak with most miraculous organ.

From the time we were girls, my sister and I had read and re-read the plays of Shakespeare. We were certain that somewhere, hidden within the words and

173

verses, we would find some small glimpse of our mother, the woman who had bore us, bestowed on us the names of two such ill-fated girls, and left the world before we ever knew her at all.

My father had entrusted my mother's well-worn books to Desi and me many years ago, and we had treasured them, poring through them each night before we climbed into our beds to sleep. Were I home, I could easily find the crimped and stained pages of Hamlet in the large tome of Shakespeare's works. Here, I could only go by memory. I closed my eyes and conjured up the words that surrounded them, the scene of which they were a part.

That this quote was written on the handkerchief covering the small murdered bird had to mean something. I shuddered as I recalled the dull eyes, its stiff feet, the painted porcelain hatpin that rested snugly in its feathered breast. There was no sign or smell to warn me of what lay beneath the linen shroud, none of the sagging flesh or bone that bespoke decomposition. Desi had been dead for nearly a month. If the bird had been there on her dressing table the night she died, it would have been much more decayed than it had seemed.

Obviously, whoever left it there expected it to be found by someone. But who was expected to enter Desi's room? The servants, Mrs. Hartley, Cade, and I were the most obvious choices, but I narrowed it down quickly to only two: Cade and I.

Dory, Mrs. Hartley, and the other servants would only be expected to be there for two reasons: should cleaning be necessary or to pack Desdemona's things away. I assumed that before her things were packed away, both Cade and I would have been expected to wander through her room, searching for memories and mementos of the woman we had known and loved.

I tried not to picture Cade alone in Desi's room, touching her things, remembering the times they'd shared, the things that had made him love her. I had found, in the years of assisting my father in his bereavement duties, that it took some spouses longer to get to that point than others. I had not seen Cade's grief, only the hurt Desi had caused before her death, but I knew somewhere inside of him was the grief of a man who had lost his wife and the mother of his child. To have lost her in such a violent and unexpected manner would, in all probability, affect the grief process in some way.

I forced myself to focus, not on Cade the grieving husband but on Cade the murder suspect. The night I chased the woman in white up to the rooftop, I'd told him our father called me his dove and Desi his barn swallow. Had he left the bird there after that, knowing I would be the one to find it? Or had he known it before Desi was killed? In my shock at finding it, had I missed the signs that it had been there longer? Why would he do such a thing?

Regardless of its target, Desi or me, the message was clear. A murderer walked the halls of Almenara.

I pulled a robe on over my nightgown and tiptoed down the hallway toward Desi's room. Through the open window, I heard Cade's voice calling out to the grooms in the stable. I watched as they brought the black stallion to him, and he swung himself up in the saddle. Within seconds, he disappeared from sight, the thundering of the horse's hooves drifting back over the dunes.

Without wasting a second, I slipped into Cade's room instead of Desi's. I inhaled the thick, warm fragrance of the soap he used, combined with the scent that was uniquely his. My eyes searched the room, trying to ignore the unmade bed and the pillow where his head had rested only moments ago. If I touched it, would it still hold his body warmth? I gave myself a mental shake, reminding myself that I was here for a reason other than fantasizing about Cade.

I had no idea what I was searching for as I opened bureau drawers and doors. I only knew I needed to find some proof of Cade's innocence, or his guilt. Feeling like a burglar, I tiptoed around the room, looking in every nook and cranny until, at last, I admitted defeat.

There was nothing here that could prove or disprove Cade's innocence, and nothing that would tell me if he had left the bird in Desi's room.

I slipped out as quietly as I had come in, and turned from the door, gasping when I came face to face with Calvin Scott.

"Good morning, Miss Garrett," he said with a leering grin.

"Good morning, Mr. Scott." Although my voice sounded calm enough, I felt the heat rise up my neck to blaze across my face.

"It is good to see you up and about," he said. "Although I must admit, I hadn't expected you to venture so far from the comfort of your own bed."

My face grew even hotter, and I was certain it was red as a beet. I made to pass him, and his hand snaked out, catching me by the arm before I could move.

"Watch yourself, Miss Garrett," he said in a voice

so low I had to strain to hear him. "You don't want to end up like your sister."

"Or your wife?" The words were out before I could stop them. I had never tried to hurt another person, physically or verbally, and I was sorry the moment I spoke.

Calvin's face went white as a sheet, and he took a step back, as if to distance himself from my hateful reminder. It was the first real emotion I had ever witnessed from him, and there was no denying the pain that darkened his eyes.

"What do you know of Amelia?"

"I only know she died the same way my sister did. I know she fell from the lighthouse."

The color rushed back to his face and his grip tightened on my arm.

"That's where you're wrong, Miss Garrett. Neither my Amelia nor your sister fell from the lighthouse. My sweet little wife threw herself over the side, and Cade threw your sister over."

"You don't know that."

"Oh, yes, I do."

"What evidence do you have?" I cried. "You'll have to prove it in court."

"I have all the evidence I need, Miss Garrett." He let go of my arm, and his usual artificial smile curved his mouth. "You see, Miss Garrett, Cade used his own cravat to tie her hands. When we found her, his collar still covered her eyes."

The air rushed out of me, leaving me slightly dizzy, but I held my ground as questions swirled through my mind. How could Cade have left those details out when he told me what happened to Desi? He had led me to believe there was no evidence against him, and that he didn't need to worry about a defense. No wonder he was so certain he needed to make arrangements for Tabitha. He had known all along that this trial was nothing but a formality. He would hang for Desdemona's murder, not because he did it, but because all the evidence pointed to him.

"Thank you for your concern, Mr. Scott," I said through my parched throat. "I will keep your warning in mind."

I had just settled down in the chair overlooking the garden when there was a light tap on the door.

"Oh, Fee, I'm so glad you're feeling better," Eleanor exclaimed as she came toward me. "You gave us all quite a fright. I thought Cade would go out of his mind before your fever broke."

"I'm feeling much better, Eleanor. Thank you for your concern."

"Of course we were concerned. You are Cade's family and therefore ours as well." She was dressed in an emerald green riding habit, trimmed with black ribbons, and as she sat in the other chair, she pulled off her matching hat and gloves.

"Have you already been riding?" I asked.

"Yes. I went out early this morning. I saw Cade down by the water. He was so deep in thought, I don't think he even saw me."

Below us, Lorraine and Calvin appeared, walking arm in arm along the winding stone path. Here and there she pointed and he nodded, continuing on until at last they came to the edge of the woods. I wondered if they were planning the future as master and mistress of the manor. Had he and Amelia done the same?

They sat together on an iron bench, and I wondered, as Lorraine smoothed her skirts and adjusted the small hat perched on her head, how she had come from being a judge's lover to Calvin's wife. Had she been content to live here in a house that was not hers, watching Desi play lady of the house for the last six years? Had the fact that she had been here longer but was not the woman who made even the most basic household decisions gnawed at her as I suspected? How had she felt when Cade came home with a wife? There did not appear to have been any love lost between her and my sister, but had she hated her for usurping what little power she might have once had or for other reasons altogether? Could she have killed her?

Hadn't Calvin himself hinted at a relationship between him and Desi? Had that merely been a ploy to infuriate Cade, or had it been true? Had they worked together to frame Cade for Desi's murder?

Eleanor gasped as Devlin came up over the dunes and lurched toward the couple.

He looked as he had the day of Desi's funeral, with Lorraine's dark blue cloak covering his clothes and his hair standing on end. How had he managed to appear so sane as we sat at Nellie's table a week ago?

Eleanor pushed the window open, ready to call out to him, but I stopped her with a hand on her arm.

"No!"

She jerked her arm away, shooting me an angry glance. Before she could speak to him, he caught sight of us at the window.

"Ophelia!" he called. "I've come to speak to you."

I shrank back, my heart pounding as I hid in the shadows.

"Ophelia, please!"

"Cade, no!" Eleanor's screech echoed through the house, as she turned from the window and rushed from the room.

I stepped in front of the window, shocked to see Cade tackle Devlin, who came up like a wild man, fists balled and face fiery red. I watched in horror as the two of them beat each other senseless. Calvin held his sister around the waist, as she kicked and fought him like a wild cat. His face turned crimson beneath her onslaught, and finally, without missing a beat, he struck her across the face. She crumpled to the ground at his feet, and Calvin stepped over her as if she were nothing but a pile of rags.

His meaty fists grasped Devlin, pulling him to his feet, and with a hard push sent him stumbling back toward the dunes.

Turning to Cade, he held out a hand and pulled him to his feet also. Cade lifted his face toward me, and I grasped the windowsill for support. His beautiful face was bruised and bloodied, but it was the crooked grin that scared the wits out of me. How could I trust a man who found pleasure in the pain he and Devlin had just inflicted on one another?

Although I barely remember packing, within an hour I stood on the porch, luggage in hand, and waited for the carriage that would take me to the train station.

In all my life I had never witnessed such violence and hatred as I had seen here at Almenara. My father had striven to give Desi and me the most peaceful of lives, and if my sister had chosen to live the last years of her life in a place of madness, that was her business. I would not live another minute of mine here. It seemed to me that most of the inhabitants of this place were driven by demons I had no desire to know.

Cade appeared on the porch beside me.

"Dory says you're leaving."

"Yes."

"Eleanor is not injured."

"That is good to know."

"Has the carriage already been summoned?"

"Yes."

"Will I ever see you again?"

"Not at Almenara."

"Calvin regrets hitting her. And I did no permanent damage to Devlin."

"I don't care."

"What happened to your compassion for all mankind?"

I turned and look into his haggard face. I tried my best to summon any feeling that would overcome my need for self-preservation. His trial loomed ahead of him, and more than likely he would be found guilty. If nothing proving his innocence came to light, he would hang within weeks and I would never see him again. It was a sign of my own shock and dismay that these facts didn't seem to faze me a bit.

"My compassion extends only so far, Cade. My sister died here, most likely murdered by someone she knew, and although you are the one who stands accused, and you are the one all the evidence points to, you are just one in a household full of people capable of it."

His face was very pale, and I felt a moment of regret at my words. "Who told you about the evidence?"

"It doesn't matter now. Make arrangements for Tabitha and Janie to be sent to me, should it come to that," I said, my voice cold and distant.

"Good-bye, Ophelia," he said quietly as he opened the carriage door for me.

I looked back once before we rounded the corner in the drive. He stood where I'd left him, a desolate and lonely man, with no one left who was convinced of his innocence.

Chapter Twenty

The cozy cottage my father and I had shared was a welcome sight, and I breathed a sigh of relief as I came through its front door late that night. Everything was endearingly familiar, still in the same place I'd left it a fortnight ago, and for the most part in the same place my father had kept it for years. There were no surprises to be found here, and for that I was profoundly grateful.

With another thankful sigh, I sank into the overstuffed chair in front of the fireplace. It felt as if I had been gone for years instead of days, and I was happy to be back where I belonged.

Music drifted through the windows, and the sound of laughter mingled with the murmur of familiar voices. The pub down the street would be overflowing with people I had known all my life. Dear, familiar people who, although far from perfect, were caring and decent and loyal to those they loved. If I went there tonight, they would raise a glass in honor of Desdemona and regale me with stories of the high-spirited girl we had all once known. They would be stories I knew by heart, containing no secrets or vile surprises. To a man, they would speak kindly of her, of me, and of our father. I would be asked to dance by the same men who had asked me a thousand times before, and when they took my hand, I would feel nothing but safe in their friendly arms.

This was a world far from the drama of Almenara, and it was the world in which I belonged. Even as I thought it, however, the memory of Cade came unbidden, and the aching loneliness of years past collided with all those yet to come.

I slept soundly, without the benefit of laudanum, for the first time in what seemed a lifetime.

I dressed for church the next morning, hoping to come and go through the back door without any of the parishioners noticing my presence. I had no desire to answer the questions I was sure my wounded visage would spark or hear the murmured condolences of people who remembered Desi as the girl they had watched grow up here.

I was lucky that John Bailey had sent Amos to pick me up from the station last night. Amos was a quiet man, caught up in the workings of his own mind, and hadn't even noticed my injuries and pallor.

If I could continue to avoid John and Mrs. Dupree, I should be able to make up an acceptable excuse for my appearance to offer the others. It was only those two who would delve deeper into anything I said and force me to either tell the truth or make up lies too elaborate for me to ever support.

I intentionally arrived several minutes late and waited until the congregation stood to sing the first hymn before sneaking in and taking a seat on the back pew. Mrs. Dupree always sat on the second row to the left, and although I couldn't see her from where I sat, I could see John and Jess Bailey standing side by side several rows away.

I stood with everyone else to sing the hymns, sat when told, and let out a sigh of relief when the preacher moved to the pulpit with his Bible. My energy and strength had not yet fully returned, and I found my eyes drifting closed several times during the sermon. When he asked that everyone stand for the last hymn, I slipped out the door.

"I hope you don't think you'll get away that easily," said Adelaide Dupree as I came around the corner. She stood beside her carriage, and I guessed she had been waiting for me for quite a while. She confirmed this by saying, "I missed the entire sermon, awaiting your exit. I know you well enough to know you thought you could sneak in and out and avoid the wild speculations and questions your banged-up face would cause."

"I really don't wish to talk about it, Mrs. Dupree."

"Well, girl, that is just too bad. You are joining me for lunch at my house, and you are going to tell me exactly what that foolish young man did to you this time."

"It wasn't him," I said, and her eyebrows rose dramatically at my quick defense of Cade.

"I'll decide if it was his fault or not, once I hear the tale. Otherwise, I'll assume he is as dastardly as they say he is, that he murdered Desdemona and injured you to boot."

I sighed in surrender, or maybe relief, I couldn't tell. All I knew was that the desire to talk about the events of the last few weeks with someone who was not directly involved suddenly seemed like a welcome idea.

I climbed up into her carriage, and within a few moments we were at her house, where she led me into the dining room. Mrs. Dupree was exceedingly punctual, and her maid had already set the table with lunch and tableware prior to our arrival.

"We'll talk while we eat," she announced. "And afterwards, my man will take you home. You seem as if you could use some rest, and even an exercise as sedate as attending church tires me out these days."

Mrs. Dupree had been well into her sixties when her husband passed away and in her early seventies when I accompanied her to New Orleans, meaning she was somewhere around eighty now. I once again told myself that I shouldn't burden her with anything but the most minimal of details regarding my time at Almenara. With that in my mind, I began my story. It wasn't until the grandfather clock in the corner struck two that I realized we had been talking for over an hour, and with her gentle prodding, she had somehow gotten every sordid detail out of me.

"I'm so sorry. I only meant to share a condensed version of what happened."

She chuckled at my obvious dismay. "Well, it needed to come out, I'd say. Besides, if I hadn't heard it all, there would be things that weren't as crystal clear as they are to me now."

I had a hard time believing anything about what I'd just told her could be crystal clear, but I was game for her observations.

"First of all, it's quite clear to me that you are even more madly in love with Cade Scott than you were in New Orleans. Second, it's quite clear to me that he feels the same way. I see that you have both found a convenient scapegoat for the time you've lost, but I don't feel that you should wear the blame alone. He was quite as guilty as you were."

Once again, I opened my mouth to come to Cade's

defense, but she lifted her hand.

"Don't give me that drivel about you choosing to leave Desdemona behind. While I can vouch for the boy's attempts to resist her charms, he failed miserably in the end. When she told him she was pregnant, he believed it to be his and married her straight away. If he was completely innocent, she'd never have been able to trap him so effectively."

I agreed, of course, but it didn't change the fact that I was in love with him, or that I truly believed he was in love with me.

"I hate to speak ill of the dead, but your sister worked her wiles on Cade, just as she did every other man she ever wanted. He missed you horribly after you'd gone, but there she was, not only looking just like you, but acting like you, too. If I hadn't known any better, I would have thought she was you for the first few weeks after your departure."

"Cade told me she was quite convincing. But, truly, all that is water under the bridge. What I need to know is what to do now."

"Well, you left him once before and absolutely no good came of it. Perhaps you should have had a bit more fortitude this time around. I doubt there's much hope of saving him, if all you say is correct, so your only decision is whether you can live with yourself if he dies alone, believing you think him guilty. I certainly can't answer that for you."

Could I live with myself if he died alone? I had seen what I considered the worst in him, but did I really believe he could have killed Desdemona? Or Amelia Scott? Or even the poor maid, Susan? I had tried to find anything that would prove to me he was innocent, and I had come up with nothing. On the other hand, the only proof he was guilty was the cravat and the collar, and those could have easily been pilfered by someone bent on casting suspicion on him. I wondered if anyone had considered that possibility or if Cade was right and they had immediately believed him guilty of Desdemona's murder because of Amelia's death years before.

"Well, my dear, I think we've reached the end of our little visit. I assume you'll let me know how you're doing in a few days' time." Mrs. Dupree pushed herself to her feet, groaning a bit at the creaking of her knees but otherwise quite spry for a woman her age. "If my health holds, I may just travel out west in the fall. Perhaps you could join me."

"Perhaps," I agreed, embracing her gently. "I shall visit with you later in the week."

"Of course," she said, but her smile told me she knew I was already contemplating a journey back to Cade's side.

Chapter Twenty-One

I arrived home feeling anxious and out of sorts. The telling of the story had not offered me any relief from my questions. Instead, they haunted me even more, for I realized that I still had not reconciled myself to Cade's guilt. Yet I had been unable to find anything to prove his innocence.

On that note, I needed to make preparations for Tabitha's arrival in my home. I had continued using my own girlhood room after my father's death, but I would now need to use it and Desi's adjoining room as the nursery suite to accommodate Tabitha and Janie. I would need to move my belongings to the large room that had been my father's. I had emptied it of his clothing and other personal belongings years ago, and it was only a matter of moving my things into the empty room.

By nightfall, I was exhausted and aching from head to toe. Both Richard and Cade would lecture me, but I had moved nearly everything from my room to my father's. Only my mother's books remained where Desi and I had kept them all these years, and I decided they could wait until morning.

I stood there in the doorway, imagining the way Desi and I had curled beneath the dormer windows, reading those very books in the moonlight. How we had giggled our secrets together and made our plans for the

189

future.

In the daylight, we often went our own ways, but here in this room, we had always come together. Now, Desi's little girl would lay her head down to dream in the moonlight that streamed through those windows. Would she miss the house where she grew up? Would she cry for her father? Would she be able to understand his absence?

How could she understand it when I, a full-grown woman, couldn't? The thought of the world emptied of Cade's presence hit me full force, and a sob forced itself from my throat.

What kind of person was I that I could have left him to face his fate alone? I had not even left him with a kind word. Instead, after all my avowals of belief in his innocence, I had thrown them in his face and walked away.

What happened to your compassion for all mankind?

His question echoed in the empty house around me. How many times had I told him I wasn't the girl he had known so many years ago? Yet he refused to see how true it was. Until the last moment we were together, that is, when I showed him exactly how deep my bitterness ran.

Chapter Twenty-Two

I slept fitfully that night, tormented by dreams filled with dead birds, funeral dirges, and Cade's lifeless eyes staring at me from a dark gaping hole at the seaside cemetery. I woke in a cold sweat, with tears streaming down my face.

I washed and dressed, and with determined steps made my way to the train station to purchase a ticket back to Almenara. On my way home, I stopped by John Bailey's office to inform him of my plans.

He stood when I entered, but after beckoning me to a chair he sat back down behind his desk.

"Fee, it's good to see you this morning." He peered at me, his sharp old eyes taking in my puffy, red-rimmed eyes and sickly pallor. "How'd you sleep your first few nights back home? It's funny how quickly we humans can get used to one place over the other."

"I slept well. It was good to be home." The first sentence was a lie, the second the truth. It was good to be home, but I would find no pleasure or peace here until I did the right thing by Cade and my niece.

"Your father always said you were a poor liar," he said with a kind smile. "He also told me your heart was broken by Cade Scott and your sister."

I thought of the many days John had sat beside my father's bed before his death, the murmur of their voices drifting down the hall. I rarely made out a word of what they were saying, but I was eternally grateful for John's presence. I should have known that after being friends for so long they would share each other's secrets, as well as mine.

"Has he done it again, Fee?" John asked. "Broken your heart?"

"No, but I'm fairly certain I broke his." My voice cracked, and John's mouth curled into a gentle bow.

"You're at a good place, then. Stuck at an impasse where forgiveness is required from both if either of you ever want to move forward again."

"I'm going back to Almenara."

"I figured as much when I saw you heading for the train station bright and early this morning."

"Could you have Amos bring a carriage around in an hour?"

"Of course. Are you sure you'll be okay there, Fee? I won't lie and say you don't look a mite worse for wear since you left us. I wouldn't be a very good friend to you or your father if I let you put yourself in harm's way."

I hadn't offered John any reason for the faint bruises and scrapes that were still visible on my face, or for my lingering pallor and frailty, and I didn't want to go into detail now. I was certain he knew of my lunch with Mrs. Dupree, and by tonight he'd know everything I'd told her.

"There's nothing to worry about," I assured him. "I contracted a fever while at Almenara, and I suppose I'm still recovering."

"Perhaps you should stay home for a while. Have Dr. Neely look you over. Rest and recuperate."

"I must get back to Cade. No matter what happens,

I intend to be at his side."

"The way I hear it, he'll most likely hang for Desi's murder, Fee. Will you be home then?" His voice was sympathetic, but held a note of worry, as well.

"Yes, but I won't be alone when I return, John. If Cade is gone, Desi's little girl will be with me. If that's the case, I'll need to arrange for the upstairs rooms to be readied for her and her nurse. I've made notes of what else needs to be done. Can you see to hiring someone, should it come to that?"

I placed my detailed list on his desk, and he took it in his hands, staring at it closely. He lifted misty eyes to mine.

"So Desdemona has a daughter, eh? And now the poor little thing will be left alone. Lucky she has you, Fee. Jess and I will take care of what needs to be done. We'll look forward to having her here, too."

"Thank you, John. I'll let you know when to expect me home."

I stood, and he moved around the desk. Perhaps we both doubted I'd ever be back, for he hugged me as tightly as my father would have, and there were tears in his eyes when we moved apart. He bid me farewell with an encouraging grin and a gentle pat on the back.

True to his word, John had a carriage waiting to take me and my suitcases back to the station within the hour. This time, my mother's books were packed within the folds of my gowns, the stained linen handkerchief flattened between the pages of Hamlet.

Chapter Twenty-Three

As the train chugged away from the platform, leaving me standing there, I looked about, surprised to find the station deserted.

From somewhere in town, I could hear the sounds of a crowd, and I hurried toward it, certain I'd find someone to take me to Almenara. My valise was much heavier with my mother's books inside, but I didn't want to risk losing it, so I carried it with me, despite its cumbersome weight.

The roar of the crowd turned into angry cries as I rounded the corner to the town square and came to a halt, my heart dropping at the sight of the mob gathered outside the church.

"Murderer!" one of the men yelled.

"He must pay!" added a woman at his side.

"No!" Eleanor screamed from somewhere at the rear of the crowd.

My eyes searched for her, finally finding her held tightly between Mrs. Hartley and Lorraine.

I called their names as I crossed the street, but I was upon them before they heard me. When they finally did, Mrs. Hartley looked as if she would burst into tears of relief.

"Praise be, miss. You're back."

"What is happening?"

"Poor little Kathleen was found dead at the

lighthouse. Some of the men have run Devlin up in the church and are demanding his arrest. After they're done with him, though, that might be pointless. It seems they're intent on killing him."

I don't know what made me push my way through the crowd. I heard Mrs. Hartley begging me not to enter the church, and some of the people outside tried to grab hold of me as I went, but I propelled my body forward, out of their grasp.

Inside the church, I found a scene straight out of hell. Men were gathered around the prone and bloodied body of the man everyone called Devlin. I don't know why, at that inexplicable moment, it dawned on me that I had no idea what his surname was, or if Devlin was his surname and it was his first that was lost to me. I could only think that if we were to bury him, we'd need to know exactly what should go on the tombstone.

The men were still hitting and kicking at him, obviously intent on finishing the fatal job they had already started.

Nellie Arnold was standing entirely too close to them, pleading with them to stop as tears streamed down her face.

I practically ran down the aisle, and taking several of the men by surprise, pushed them away, until I was standing between them and the unconscious man.

"Move out of the way, miss," one of them grumbled, but I shook my head.

"I won't stand by and let you kill him." My voice was surprisingly steady given the horror that raced through me.

"He's killed our girls, he has. Nearly killed you, as well."

"He did nothing of the kind," I said. "He left me alone at the lighthouse, yes, but my life was never in danger."

It might have been a lie, I wasn't sure. At the time, I'd felt certain I was in mortal peril, but I denied it now with far more bravado than I felt.

"What proof do you have that he killed those girls?"

"He was there, miss, picking our Kathleen's pockets after she was dead."

I shuddered at the thought but tried not to let it sway my resolve to prevent another murder from taking place.

"He told you he found her after her murder," Nellie moaned, wrapping an arm around her belly. "Why won't you believe him?"

A chorus of voices sounded at the gruesome idea, and they surged forward once again.

"Stay back!" I ordered, moving even closer to Devlin and giving Nellie a gentle nudge toward the nearest pew. "Nellie, sit down!"

"Why should we listen to you?" snarled a young man I recognized as the blacksmith's son. "We all know what your sister was, and there's nothing saying you aren't just the same. Now she's dead, killed at the hands of her husband, and you stand over her lover like a common harlot."

I tried to protest his judgment but was cut short by Kathleen's father.

"We don't want to hear it, miss. There's a job to finish, and we're going to finish it right here and now."

A booted foot struck out at Devlin, but my shin caught the brunt of it, and I gasped with pain. Some of the men stepped back then, clearly unwilling to do me harm, but others stepped forward to take their places, and I was dismayed at the bloodlust in their eyes.

"The sheriff's coming!" a woman called from the church door, and I breathed a sigh of relief. I might not care to be around the surly man, but I was glad to know he was on his way to put an end to this madness.

"Might as well get it done then," one of the men said. He raised a wooden stick high above his head, and as he brought it down, I had no choice but to protect the poor unconscious man from the blow. The stick caught me across the shoulders and back, and I cried out as pain exploded through my body.

"Hey, now!" Kathleen's father yelled. "No need to harm the lady."

It seemed his defense of me was the spark that ignited a melee, and I curled myself into a ball, protecting myself as best I could from the heavy boots that flew around me. Several caught me in various parts of my body, and by the time Calvin, Dennis, and several other levelheaded men broke up the fight, I was dizzy and nauseous with pain.

Dr. Scarborough entered then, ordering Nellie home and to bed immediately. "There's not a doubt in my mind that baby will be here tonight, so I'll be up to your house as soon as I've seen to Devlin."

"We'll see to Devlin up at Almenara," Calvin informed him, as Nellie cried out from the doorway. "You'd best see to Mrs. Arnold."

"I'll be up to check on him after she delivers," Richard agreed, paying me no mind. "I doubt anything but time will heal his injuries, although there may be some bones I need to set."

"Dennis, get Devlin up to the house," Calvin ordered. "He's in no shape to be jailed or even questioned. I'll keep him there until he's healed.

"Should I carry Fee up, as well?" Dennis asked, studying me worriedly.

"No, I'll see to her myself."

He didn't say anything to me, just scooped me up as if I weighed nothing and carried me away from the church. I expected to be placed in the same wagon that was carrying Devlin to Almenara, but Calvin passed it by and headed down the street.

My head throbbed, one eye was swollen nearly closed, and I could feel a slow trickle of blood from the reopened cut on my forehead. I hurt from head to toe and, quite truthfully, kept from swooning only by sheer force of will.

"Am I under arrest?" I asked as we passed through the doors to his office, then the jail beyond. My words sounded so slurred I wasn't sure he'd understood me until I heard him chuckle.

"You should be, but I can't arrest people for being stupid."

He unlocked a cell and deposited me on a small cot.

"This woman is a damn fool," he said, his eyes on the darkened corner of the room.

"What the devil happened?" Cade demanded, stepping into the light.

"She tried to break up a lynching," Calvin said, before I could answer. "Apparently someone hit her, she went down, and all hell broke loose."

"Ophelia, you could have been killed."

The fight seemed to leave me, and I leaned heavily

against the wall behind me.

Cade moved to sit beside me, gathering me against him as Calvin bid us farewell and slid the door closed behind him. I am certain I was asleep before he was outside the building.

Chapter Twenty-Four

The sun coming through the single window woke me, and I turned into a strong masculine chest.

My swollen eyes opened as much as possible, and I stared into Cade's worried face.

He cupped my cheek gently. "I could kill them all for this."

"They are angry and afraid. They've lost three girls already and are afraid of losing more."

"But you're an innocent. They had no right to harm you."

"I stood between them and the one they blame."

"Devlin." He spit the word out like poison.

"Yes."

"Why did you protect him?"

"I had to. Compassion for all mankind, you know. My father would have it no other way."

He was quiet, no doubt remembering our last conversation.

"Your father is long dead."

"But his teaching lives in me."

"I doubt he would have wanted you to help at the risk of being hurt."

"He wouldn't have stood in my way if I thought what I was doing was right."

"Is that always what guides you, Fee? What you believe is right?"

"I hope so."

"What if you're wrong?"

I looked at him, lying in a narrow prison bed, his eyes filled with sadness, his mouth bracketed by worry. All those years ago, I had done what I thought was right. I had set what I wanted aside and left him behind to care for my father because I felt it was the right thing to do. I had suspected the cause of my sister's illness, I finally admitted to myself, and I had hoped she would find a man to care for her and her child. I had never thought it would be Cade, but perhaps I hadn't thought about anything at all, except what I thought was right for all of us. All these years, I had clung to the belief that I had made the right decision, and I had covered myself in righteous anger that I had been betrayed because of it. Now I could see the possibility that I had been wrong. Perhaps what I'd done had not been the right thing at all. Perhaps I should have made Desi return home to help take care of our father and mend the damage she'd done. Perhaps I should have been honest with Cade, told him what I suspected and promised to come back to him. Instead, I'd sentenced us all to a life of unhappiness because I thought I was the best judge of how we all should proceed with our lives.

"I was wrong to leave Almenara," I told him now, resting my hand on his cheek. "And I was wrong to leave you in New Orleans. If I had stayed, all those years ago, everything would have been so different."

"All these years I could have known happiness in your arms." He kissed my forehead softly. "Now it's too late."

I shook my head. "It's never too late."

He laughed softly, bitterly. "We both know that's not true, Fee. We'd be lying to ourselves to think we have a future of happiness ahead of us. I'm going to hang in a few weeks' time, and you're going to return to your home, my daughter in tow."

"If Devlin killed Susan and Kathleen, couldn't that mean he killed Desi, too?"

"We have no proof he killed any of them, Fee, and unless we can prove it, I won't let him take the blame for it."

"But you're willing to take the blame for it? To hang for murders you didn't commit?" I cried. "Why are you so willing to die?"

"I thought you doubted my innocence."

He killed her, Ophelia. I watched him do it.

Should I tell him what Devlin had said? How would he react? Should I wait until Calvin returned? I shook my head. Did I really believe Cade would lose his temper and harm me in an attempt to keep me silent about what Devlin had told me? How could I possibly take the word of a madman over Cade's claims of innocence? I had come back so certain of what I believed, but even now the words Devlin had whispered in my ear were powerful enough to give me pause.

Cade's voice was soft, tired and disappointed. "Why did you come back?"

"I didn't want you to be alone."

"Even if I killed your sister?"

I nodded, and a sob caught me off guard. "I'm sorry, Cade. I'm so sorry."

He got up and moved to the other side of the cell, his pain palpable in the small space between us.

"Calvin received word that the judge is caught up

in another trial," he informed me in a dull monotone I hardly recognized as his. "He won't be in town until the day after tomorrow. There's no need for you to sit through it. You were right when you left, and it does neither of us any good for you to be here now. Go home, Fee, and take Tabby with you. I've already given the paperwork to Calvin. They know she's yours now."

I held my tongue as I stood. My body was stiff from the beating I'd endured and the night on the small uncomfortable cot, but I stifled my groan. I washed up in the basin of tepid water and tidied my hair to the best of my ability without the benefit of a mirror or comb. Let him make of my silence what he would. I knew my lingering uncertainty hurt him, but I could not change the fact that there was still some small part of me plagued by Devlin's words. Therefore, I remained silent, unwilling to injure him more than I already had.

When Calvin arrived, he unlocked the cell and let me out.

"Dennis is waiting outside. He'll give you a ride to Almenara," he told me. "Try to stay out of trouble."

"Thank you, Sheriff," I said as I followed him down the hall. "Have you had any word about Nellie?"

"According to the doctor, she delivered a healthy baby girl last night. Those are all the details I know."

"Was the doctor there to see Devlin this morning?"

"He came straight from the Arnolds' place last night. He diagnosed broken ribs, a concussion, and too many bruises to count. Said he'll be in pain for a few days but should recover."

"I'll help look after him during his recuperation."

Calvin chuckled dryly. "Eleanor's with him now, and she'll protest it, of course, but I'm sure when he wakes up he'll be grateful for your presence. I believe he finds my sister's obsession a bit overwhelming."

"Do you think he killed Kathleen?" I asked.

He shook his head.

"No, that's something Cade and I agree on. Devlin's mad as a hatter, but he certainly isn't mad enough to kill for no reason. Kathleen was dead when he found her. His only crime was being deranged enough to pick her pockets."

"Do you have any suspects?"

"Don't need any suspects. I already know who did it."

"Really? Who?"

He jerked his head toward the corridor we had just exited. "Cade."

Nothing he could have said could have brought me to my senses faster. I opened my mouth to argue, but what came out was a fit of wild laughter that caused him to step back quickly.

"Fee?" Cade yelled from down the hall. I heard the concern in his voice, and I knew I must sound like a raving lunatic. "Ophelia?"

"What's wrong with you?" Calvin eyed me uncertainly. "Have you lost your mind?"

"No," I said. "As a matter of fact, I'm thinking more clearly than I have in days."

"Fee?" Cade rattled the bars of the cell, and I ran back down the hall toward him. Once there, I grabbed his face through the bars and kissed him swiftly.

"I'm sorry, Cade," I said. "I know you didn't kill Desi or anyone else, and I'm going to prove it."

He grabbed my wrist, worry evident in his voice as he said, "Leave it alone, Fee."

I shook my head and turned to Calvin, who had followed me down the hall. "You know as well as I do that Cade didn't kill my sister, and he certainly didn't kill those other two girls. I know what you stand to gain by his imprisonment or death, and quite honestly I have never seen such a flagrant and intentional miscarriage of justice. It should be you in that cell instead of him."

"You don't know what you're talking about," he huffed, but his reddened face told me I'd hit a nerve.

"I know exactly what I'm talking about, and so do you."

I marched down the hall, leaving both men staring after me in surprise.

Outside the sheriff's office, Dennis Ames was standing behind the wagon.

"Good morning, Fee," he said, tipping his hat, and sauntering toward me.

I bid him good morning and climbed into the wagon without waiting for his help.

"In a hurry this morning?" he asked as he settled beside me on the seat.

"I can hardly wait to see Tabitha. I've missed her while I was gone." I had decided against telling anyone else I was trying to prove Cade innocent, even Dennis.

"She's pretty special, huh?" he observed.

"Yes, she is."

"Desi was awfully fond of her."

It seemed a silly statement. Of course Desi was fond of her daughter. Still, his familiarity led me to question how well he had known Desi.

"Were you and my sister very close?" I asked, remembering the other times he had intimated that Desi shared things with him she didn't share with others.

"I was her friend, if that's what you're asking," he said, sounding a bit offended at the question. "As I'm sure you realized, none of the Scotts liked her much, not even Cade. Desi was lonely, and she and I became friends soon after she arrived at Almenara."

"I meant no offense, Dennis. It simply seems to me that you knew Desi better than most. After all, you are one of only three people who even knew of my existence before I arrived at Almenara."

"I think she was embarrassed by what she did to you. Stealing Cade away like that, tricking him into marriage. She needed to confess to someone, and I was the one she chose."

My shock must have shown on my face, because he laughed lightly as he urged the horses to pick up speed.

"I guess you could say I was Desi's confidant, and I hope I helped ease her mind before she died."

"I'm sure having such a good, loyal friend put her mind very much at ease." I touched his arm and offered him a smile. "Thank you."

"It was my pleasure." He snapped the reins and the horses leapt forward.

Richard's carriage was in the drive when we arrived at Almenara, and I supposed he was there checking up on Devlin. I had been surprised that he hadn't even asked after me when he entered the church last night, but I supposed he could see by looking at me that I had no serious injuries. It had been Nellie who was of the highest concern, and I understood that completely.

Mrs. Hartley greeted us in the hall and, at my inquiry, directed me to the room in which Devlin was convalescing. I felt a leap of anxiety over the idea of sleeping under the same roof as the man, but when I remembered the beating he had taken the day before, I realized it would be quite some time before he could be a danger to anyone.

Dennis followed me up the stairs, much more somber than I had ever seen him, and by the time we entered Devlin's room, he seemed to have transformed into another man entirely. A scowling avenger, come to reap his pound of flesh from the bruised and beaten man lying against the crisp white sheets.

"He's resting comfortably," Richard said as we entered.

"Then we won't disturb him," I said, turning away from the sleeping man and expecting Dennis would follow.

"Of course we'll disturb him," Dennis protested. "He has questions to answer."

"And he can answer them when he wakes," the doctor told him sternly.

Dennis ignored the man completely, however, as he slapped his hand against Devlin's covered foot with more force than necessary and shouted at him to wake up.

At the command, Devlin's black and swollen eyes fluttered partially open and settled on me.

Richard ordered Dennis to follow him from the room and Dennis obeyed, although he looked back at Devlin and me several times.

"My God, Desdemona, what's happened to me?" Devlin croaked. "I hurt like the devil."

I wanted to tell him I wasn't Desdemona but had the idea that I could lure the truth from him if I pretended to be her.

I tried to emulate the way she talked, the way her hips swayed when she walked and how she cocked her head closer to men when speaking to them.

"You were set upon and beaten by a group of men," I said, sounding like my sister even to my own ears.

"Why? Where?" Confusion knitted his brow.

"Perhaps you should rest, Devlin," I suggested.

"Perhaps I should," he agreed, "but I'd rather talk."

The short shallow gasps that punctuated his speech made me wonder how many broken ribs the doctor had found beneath the clean white shirt he wore.

I felt infinitely sorry for the man, mad as he was, and I reached for his hand. It was a gesture of comfort, but because he thought I was my sister, his hand curled around mine and held it tight.

"Where is Cade?" he asked, his eyes searching the room, as if a man of Cade's stature could be hiding in the corners.

"He isn't home." I couldn't tell him where Cade was. If I did, I would have to explain why, which would make him realize I couldn't possibly be Desdemona.

As if that was all he had been waiting for, he gave my hand a gentle tug so I was forced closer to him, grasped my head and pulled me down for a kiss. I tried to pull away from him, Desi's soft laughter spilling from my lips as I put a few inches between our mouths.

"You shouldn't overexert yourself, Devlin. The doctor says you must rest."

"I'll rest when I'm dead," he murmured against my mouth, "but right now, I refuse."

He pulled me against him again, and it was at that

moment that the door opened and Dennis came back into the room.

"What the—" He cut himself short and rushed toward the bed.

"No, Dennis, wait!" I cried, catching hold of his arm. "It isn't what you think."

"It is exactly what he thinks, Desdemona," Devlin said from behind me. "It's time for this charade to be over."

"Desdemona?" Dennis repeated, his eyes swinging to mine.

I nodded, hoping he understood and hoping Devlin didn't notice his questioning gaze.

"Do you know this man?" Devlin asked me, his brow knitted with worry.

"Dennis is my dearest friend," I answered. "I'm sure the two of you have met each other before."

"I'm sorry, but I don't seem to remember," Devlin apologized.

A slow heat spread across Dennis' face, and he seemed to puff up before my eyes.

"We've met numerous times, sir," Dennis snapped, but Devlin shook his head.

"Again, it isn't something I recall." He waved a weak hand toward the door. "If you would be so kind, Desdemona and I have things to discuss in private."

I had never seen Dennis as anything but a sweet congenial gentleman, and the change that came over him was as frightening as it was fascinating. His face mottled with rage, he stepped toward the bed, and spoke in a voice tight with fury.

"Maybe you'll remember who I am when I arrest you for murder."

"Murder? Whose murder?" Devlin looked at me, then Dennis. "Are you the sheriff, then?"

"I think we've played your game long enough." Dennis put a hand on his arm. "You know I'm not the sheriff, and you know we've met before."

"Are you mad, man?"

Dennis lifted his fist, intent on connecting with Devlin's face, and for the second time in as many days I stepped between Devlin and a devastating blow.

My backside was pressed firmly against the side of the bed as Dennis caught his swing in midair and, cursing wildly, grabbed my arm to drag me from the room.

"What the devil is wrong with you?" he demanded once we were in the hall. "That man may have killed your sister and two other innocent girls. Why are you so intent on saving him from injury?"

Appalled and infuriated, I straightened my spine and held my ground. "That man is in no shape to defend himself, physically or legally, and I won't let you hurt or question him."

"He seemed in good enough shape to kiss you. Which, I must say, you didn't seem to be protesting."

"He's delirious, Dennis. He thinks I'm my sister."

"Why don't you tell him the truth?"

"Other than thinking I'm Desi, he seems so sane at the moment that I'm afraid to tell him the truth. I don't know what he would do if he learned of Desi's death."

"You're right to be afraid. He's a dangerous man."

"If he thinks I'm Desi, he may say something that proves he killed her, or at least, that Cade is innocent."

"Cade will be furious if he learns what you're doing."

"He's the reason I'm doing it."

I went back into the bedroom and found Devlin sleeping soundly once again. Dennis had obviously calmed during our conversation, because when I turned to leave, he followed silently in my wake.

I bid him farewell in the hall and he leaned toward me, his lips brushing my cheek with a gentle kiss.

"See you tomorrow, Fee."

Chapter Twenty-Five

I ate dinner in the nursery with Tabitha that night, only halfway listening as Janie rattled on about the rumors that were going around in town. It seemed three murders in just as many weeks had not only sparked the vigilantes last night, but had set the rumor mill afire.

"Some of them are saying Mr. Devlin is a devil, miss, a heathen come to steal away the souls of women."

"Well, that is simply ridiculous, Janie."

"Kathleen's granny says he stole Mr. Cade's soul years ago, and that's why Miss Tabby is how she is. She says it's the mark of the devil."

Outraged, I surged to my feet. I could feel my anger suffuse my face with heat, and Janie sat back on her heels.

"Don't you ever again speak such nonsense in my presence. Do you understand me?"

She nodded. "It isn't like I believed it, miss."

"Maybe not, but repeating it is just as bad. Tabitha is as God made her, Cade's soul is right where it belongs, and Devlin is simply a man whose mind is ill."

"I'm very sorry, miss," she said, her eyes huge with worry. "You will still let me come away with you, won't you? I love Miss Tabby, and I could never believe she has the mark of the devil."

"I can't abide hatefulness, Janie. Especially when

aimed against an innocent child. If Kathleen's grandmother is given to such imaginings, no wonder her poor granddaughter was so superstitious."

"Have you heard her, miss?" Janie asked in a rush. "The crying woman?"

There was really no reason to lie. Everyone here had seen me rush to the rooftop in search of a woman who was nowhere in sight.

"Yes," I said. "I've heard her."

"Is it true you've seen her, too, miss? That you followed her onto the roof the night you were hurt at the lighthouse?"

"Yes, that's true, too, Janie."

"Kathleen's grandma says if you've heard her and seen her, she's got you in her sights. You could be the next one, miss, and then poor Tabby would be all alone."

"No one has me in their sights, Janie. I'm sure there's a perfectly logical explanation for all of it."

"My mama said the same thing, miss, when I told her how worried I was about you." She dabbed a napkin over Tabitha's face, gently wiping away any trace of the yams and chicken soup the child had consumed. "But that was before Kathleen saw the woman in white."

"Kathleen saw the woman?" I'm sure my relief showed on my face. I had not even admitted to myself how frightened I was at the idea that I could have imagined the woman in the hallway. "When? Where?"

"She saw her the night before she died. After you left that day, Mr. Cade locked himself away in his study. He started drinking something fierce, and when he drank all he had in there with him, he started yelling for more. Kathleen took it in to him, and the first time everything was fine. But the second time she went in, she came out white as a sheet, claiming she'd seen the woman in white outside Mr. Cade's window."

"Did she see her face?"

Janie shook her head as she picked Tabby up and changed her into her nightgown.

"She disappeared over the dunes before Kathleen got a good glimpse of her."

"Was she certain she saw her? What about Cade?" I held out my arms and she placed Tabitha on my lap.

"Oh, yes. She was quite sure, miss. But Mr. Cade didn't see a thing. Or if he did, he didn't say so. Kathleen was still out of sorts the next morning, saying Mrs. Scott's crying woke her in the night."

"That was the day she died?"

Janie's face fell and tears sprang to her eyes. "They found her body just before nightfall."

"And you think the woman had something to do with her death?"

"Kath's granny says the woman in white came to warn her that death was coming." Her face was earnest and concerned as she met my gaze. "You must be careful, Miss Garrett. In case the woman came to warn you, too."

"Thank you for your concern, Janie, but I don't expect anything will happen to me."

"Perhaps she's warning us all of Mr. Cade's death, miss. They say he'll hang for Mrs. Scott's murder."

"He'll stand trial first, and we can only pray they will find him innocent."

"I just can't believe a man who would love Miss Tabby like he does could kill someone."

I agreed with her assessment, but his love for Tabby was the motive behind the murder, if everything I'd heard was to be believed. It alone was the reason he'd threatened to kill her to begin with.

I looked down at the child who had fallen asleep in my arms, and love for her welled up within me. I had known her only a few weeks, yet I knew I would lay down my life for her. How much more willing would the man who was her father be to die for her? Would he really have killed to keep her here? Was Desdemona's threat to leave real, or had she only used it as a way to hurt him?

I kissed Tabitha gently, laid her in bed, and bid Janie good night before tiptoeing down the stairs to Desi's morning room. I could hear Lorraine and Calvin playing a card game down the hall, and I had seen Eleanor go into Devlin's room earlier. I was free to search Desi's space uninterrupted.

Taking a seat at the secretary, I searched her calendar, her drawers, her books, anything I could find, for any sign of what her life as mistress of Almenara had been like, who might have killed her, or what might have frightened her in the days before her death. Judging from the blank pages of her books and calendars, it appeared her duties had been limited and she'd had very few real responsibilities here. When I had exhausted every avenue in my search for answers and the clock in the hallway was striking one in the morning, I went upstairs to my room.

I fell asleep as soon as my head hit the pillow, only to be startled awake a few hours later by a dream I couldn't remember. As I fought to calm the frantic pounding of my heart, I heard the muffled but familiar sound of a woman sobbing.

Shivering with apprehension, I donned my robe and followed the sound down the nursery hall, finally stopping in front of the door that led to the roof.

Nerves made my breathing shaky as I crept up the stairs and crossed the rooftop to stand beside the huge copper cistern. Like the last time I'd followed the ghostly specter, there was no one in sight, and I turned to go inside.

The small mourning dove resting in front of the open door stopped me in my tracks. How had I missed her when I came outside? Her wing was bent at an odd angle and I scooped her up, cupping her in my hands as I went inside.

"Mr. Devlin's calling for you, Miss Fee," Dory called to me from the end of the hall.

"For me?" I asked in order to clarify what part I was to play when I entered his room. I had advised the people who would be involved with him that they were not to inform him of Desdemona's death. The doctor had agreed that it was best that we not force him to accept what his mind denied.

"No, he's calling for your sister."

I entered the room as Desi, the bird still cupped in my hands. "Dory says you were calling for me, darling."

He was half asleep, the strong doses of medicine Richard had given him taking their toll, but he reached out his hand to pet the bird.

"You and your birds," he said lovingly, an indulgent smile playing about his mouth.

"I found her on the roof. She's very young, I think."

"A dove like your sweet Ophelia."

"Yes." Tears pricked my eyes when I realized Desi must have spoken kindly of me to him.

"I heard you crying." His words were slurred, and I wondered if I'd heard him correctly. "In the hall."

A chill went up my spine at his acknowledgment of the ghostly sobs.

"It wasn't me," I whispered.

"It was Desdemona." The words were barely out of his mouth before he was asleep once more, leaving me to wonder if he had seen through my charade and why he thought he heard Desi crying.

Chapter Twenty-Six

The next morning, I was determined to talk Cade into hiring an attorney to defend him. I could hardly wait to question Calvin Scott on why he would still think Cade had killed the women when he was obviously arrested before Kathleen's body was even found.

After I dressed, I fed and watered the little dove, which seemed happy enough in an empty hatbox I pilfered from Desi's room.

As I walked past Devlin's room on my way downstairs, I peeked inside.

He was awake, propped up in bed and letting Eleanor spoon broth into his mouth. He seemed relieved when I entered the room, and shook his head when she lifted the spoon once more.

"Devlin, you must eat a bit more," she cajoled. "It will help build your strength."

"I have eaten enough, Eleanor. Now be a good girl and let me alone for a while."

"Of course. I'll just tidy up your room."

"No, I mean leave me alone, as in leave the room."

"Oh, yes. I'll run your tray to the kitchen. I'll be back in a few minutes."

"Give me an hour, woman!" he exclaimed. "I am not so unwell that I will die in that amount of time, but I am certainly not in such good health that I could do anything more than talk to a woman."

I blushed as he grinned at me, and Eleanor hurried from the room. When she was out of earshot, he spoke, and I was surprised that he seemed so lucid.

He crooked his finger toward me and I went to him, perching on the edge of the bed, as he ran his hands over my face and hair. His eyes searched mine, and with a small moan, he kissed me. It was a probing, searching kiss, and I felt nothing save pity for the man.

"You really aren't her," he sighed, tears spilling from his eyes. "She truly is dead."

"What gave me away?"

"I suspected it when I kissed you yesterday, but I contributed the lack of fire to my injuries. Today I feel much better, I have refused all but a small amount of laudanum, and I'm certain. You aren't Desdemona. You are quite adept at acting like her, but you missed some of her more endearing nuances and added one of your own. Your blush at my words to Eleanor sealed my certainty."

"But you kissed me again."

"It couldn't hurt to be sure there was no fire."

I felt myself turn red again, and he smiled sadly.

"Do you have a pencil and paper?" he asked, glancing around the room.

I rummaged through several drawers of the small writing table in front of the window before finding the items he asked for and handing them to him.

He began to draw with quick slices of the pencil, as he spoke.

"The difference in you and Desdemona is your perspective. People like you and Cade see everything in straight bold lines, like this." He turned the paper to show me what he'd drawn. The view of the lighthouse from the shore behind Almenara was quite realistic.

As he continued talking, he began moving the pencil over the paper in softer movements, occasionally rubbing a finger or eraser here or there across the paper. "Desi, on the other hand, saw softer lines. She realized that smudging a line here and there wasn't the end of the world. You have always been in a box of straight lines, while she flew outside the box, seeing the world from a bird's-eye view."

He turned the picture around and I gasped. By taking the same picture, removing some of the bold lines, adding some softer ones, and smudging them here and there, he had turned it into a view from the parapet of the lighthouse. On the rocks below, a swallow and a mourning dove sat side by side.

"It's amazing that two creatures so similar could be so different," he observed. "Two girls borne by the same woman, raised by the same man, but seeing life in such different ways."

"It was always that way."

"Yes, she told me. She wondered how different things would have been had your mother lived. She felt certain they shared a kindred spirit like you and your father did."

"I've often thought the same thing. Perhaps my mother would have seen things from Desi's perspective."

He smiled. "I told you once that I wouldn't tell you what I knew until you forgave your sister. Have you forgiven her?"

"I've come to accept that I played a role in what happened between us," I answered, knowing it wasn't the answer he was seeking, but it was the closest thing to the truth I could offer him.

"That's a huge step for you, Ophelia."

"Yes."

"You will forgive her soon," he proclaimed, "and you'll forgive yourself. Then you'll be free to face your future."

"My future is with Cade."

"And Cade will hang."

"Yes."

"I told you I watched Cade kill her."

"Yes." I waited breathlessly.

"I didn't mean it as literally as you may have taken it."

What did that mean? What metaphoric meaning could his words possibly have? It didn't matter, really, for a well of hope sprang up inside of me as he went on.

"I didn't see who threw her from the lighthouse, Fee, and, honestly, I find it impossible to imagine Cade doing such a thing. The view I had of her murder was murky at best, and when I found her, she was already dead, as was young Kathleen. What I saw Cade do was drive her there to that lonely, dangerous spot where she died, high above the rest of us, like a princess in a tower, with no one to rescue her. Their marriage was doomed from the moment they met, and their regret and disillusionment created a wall between them that was impossible for either of them to scale, even if they wanted to. Neither of them ever got over the pain they caused you. He pushed her away, and she ran into the arms of other men, always seeking the absolution no one else could give her. Before me, I don't think she had ever truly been loved."

"Cade told me he had never seen her as happy as she was during your time together."

His eyes filled with tears once more, but he smiled and nodded his head. "I am glad I was able to give her that. I loved her as I've never loved another."

Eleanor entered the room at that moment, and I stood to leave. As I turned to the door, Devlin called my name.

"I am truly sorry I hurt you, Ophelia."

"Thank you for telling me the truth," I said, and left the room with a much lighter heart.

I hardly recognized Dennis when I met him on the stairs. His shoulders were hunched, his steps heavy, and his face was a pale mask of gloom.

"Are you well, Dennis?" I asked in concern, and he nodded sharply.

"Yes, why shouldn't I be?"

"You just seem out of sorts. Are you here to see Devlin?"

"The sheriff has ordered me to play nursemaid. I'll be here looking after him all morning."

"Well, it shouldn't be too difficult, as Eleanor is doing a fine job of it already."

"Calvin said if you're ready, he'll give you a ride into town."

"Wonderful! Try to have a good day, Dennis."

Chapter Twenty-Seven

"How long will you keep up this farce?" I demanded as I rode beside Calvin on the seat of the wagon. He had received word earlier that the judge was still detained, and his face was a dark mask of frustration. "You know Cade didn't kill Kathleen and Susan."

He gave me a sidelong glance. "He wasn't arrested for killing them, Miss Garrett. He was arrested for killing his wife."

"But those girls were killed the same way she was."

"Yes, they were. Or maybe they threw themselves over. Neither of them was bound as Desdemona was."

"Two young girls threw themselves to their deaths within days of each other? Why? Young women don't do such things for no reason, Mr. Scott, and neither of them seemed unhappy."

He was silent for a moment, allowing me to ponder the cruelty of my observations. A month ago I would never have thought I could say something to another human that I knew would open a wound, but since coming to Almenara I had been a different person. I wasn't sure I liked the woman I had become, and I wondered if Desdemona had felt the same.

"I'm so sorry," I said softly, laying a hand on his arm. "It was a careless observance."

223

"No," he answered. "You're right. Amelia was unhappy and ill. I blame Cade for her death, but contrary to popular belief, I never suspected he killed her."

"He didn't kill my sister either."

He shrugged.

"He's the only suspect I have, Miss Garrett. All the evidence points to him, and like I've told you, he is the only one with a motive."

"Were you really sleeping with my sister?"

"No," he said, his eyes meeting mine. "Lorraine is all the woman I need."

Something about the words and the way he said them, touched me deeply, and I blinked back the sudden prick of tears.

"Mr. Scott, you aren't nearly as awful as you pretend to be," I proclaimed. "You have no reason to want Cade dead, and I expect you'll help me talk him into hiring an attorney to defend him. Then, you'll begin the search for the person who killed those girls, because I truly believe the person who killed them is the person who killed Desdemona."

He shook his head in exasperation. "I'll be looking for the truth about their deaths, but it won't change Cade's fate. Like I said, he wasn't arrested for their murders."

"He's your cousin."

A harsh laugh rumbled from his chest. "I'm not the first person to have a murderer in their family tree, Miss Garrett, and I doubt I'll be the last."

We rode the rest of the way in silence, but when I would have jumped down, his hands encircled my waist and he lifted me down effortlessly.

I hurried toward the jailhouse door, but he called my name, and I stopped and turned back to him.

"Be careful, Miss Garrett," he said softly, with what I though was real concern. "If Cade didn't kill Desdemona, I doubt the man who did will be pleased with your meddling."

I nodded in agreement before hurrying to the cell where Cade was being held. He lay on his back on the hard cot, shirtsleeves rolled up to his elbows. His strong tan arms were crossed over his face, covering all but his dark hair and the stubble that grew on his chin. Sunlight streamed through the small high window, glinting off the skin of his chest, where he had unfastened several of the buttons of his shirt. Desire strummed through my veins, and I called his name rather more breathlessly than I intended.

"Cade?"

He made no move, either at my soft greeting or the sound of Calvin unlocking the door and letting me in. I went toward him, laying a hand on his arm. He opened his eyes, and the dark pools of hopelessness made my breath catch in my throat. I whispered his name again, this time more a plea than a question. I needed him to believe we would find the truth. I needed him to find hope in the future.

"Go home, Fee," he said quietly as Calvin's footsteps grew farther away. "There's no need for you to witness it. Take my daughter and leave this place. Find someone who will love you both after I'm gone."

He took a shuddering breath and closed his eyes, pain etching itself into his face and voice.

"Richard Scarborough is a fine man, Fee. He loves Tabitha and I can see his attraction to you. Marry him

225

when he asks, Fee. He'll make you happy enough."

"You fool," I cried, dropping to my knees beside him. "I don't want to be happy enough. I want you. Can't you understand? That's all I've ever wanted."

He growled out an indecipherable word as one arm shot out and caught the back of my neck, pulling me into his embrace. His lips caught mine in a kiss that turned my world on its ear. I answered his growl with a purr of my own as his tongue teased mine, and his lips melded against my own.

My body's reaction was so swift and powerful, I had little knowledge of how I came to be on the cot with him, my body pressed against his as his free hand caressed my breast through the taffeta dress. I shoved my hands beneath his shirt, running them across the smooth contours of his chest and torso. Each move of my hand sent a shiver through him, and I felt drunk on the power of eliciting such a response.

"We can't do this here," he murmured when my leg slid across his as if I would straddle him. His voice was tight and pained, but I ignored it all as I drank in his panting breaths and continued my exploration.

I was silent, oblivious to the world around us, as we caressed each other, exploring areas we had never dared before. I had never felt as alive as I did there in his arms, and I knew only that I never wanted it to end.

The sound of footsteps down the hall echoed through the cell and Cade sat up quickly, bringing me with him, while pushing me away at the same time. I staggered upright, my legs wobbly as a colt's, and watched through a daze of lingering passion as he jammed his shirt back into his pants and raked a trembling hand through his hair, which sprang back up as if he'd never attempted to calm it at all.

"Lunch time," Dennis called from the other side of the bars, although the door had not been locked behind me when I entered.

His eyes narrowed, making me wonder just how disheveled I looked. I offered him a smile as I pulled the pins from my hair and began to pin it in a looser chignon than usual as I spoke.

"How are you this afternoon, Dennis? Relieved of your nursemaid duties, I see."

"If you must know, Fee, I'm really not all that well today. I had a hard time sleeping last night, thinking about you up there at Almenara letting that madman think you were Desdemona." His eyes snapped to Cade and then back to me. "He and Desdemona did far more than share a few kisses, and it bothered me all night that he might try that with you, too."

"Do you mean he tried to kiss her?" Cade spoke from behind me, in a voice gone cold with fury.

"He did more than try, I'd say."

"Fee?"

"He thought I was Desi, Cade. He kissed me, but it was nothing. I couldn't make a scene about it, because I wanted him to think I was her. By this morning, he knew I wasn't, and I knew he couldn't have killed her."

"For God's sake, Ophelia, are you trying to get yourself killed?" Cade demanded.

"Devlin is acting so sane, Cade," I argued. "I can't quite reconcile him with the lunatic I met before. But I'm left with a dilemma. He loved Desi so much and was so maddened with grief, it is nearly impossible for me to think he killed her."

"Fee, you need to stop this madness. It's a

227

dangerous game you're playing, trying to track a murderer." His voice was urgent as he stood and grasped my shoulders. "Devlin may well be sane from here on out, but on the other hand, he may lose his grasp on sanity again at any moment. And if he isn't the killer, if the killer is someone else entirely, you could be in even more danger."

"I can't stop, Cade. I know you aren't a murderer, and the good Lord has blessed me with a few extra days to prove it. I promise I will have you out of here before the judge arrives in town."

"After he realized you weren't Desi, what happened?"

"He told me what he knew about Desi's death."

"What did he tell you?" Dennis inquired, reminding me he was there.

"He told me he hadn't witnessed Cade murder her."

"Did he see her murder?"

"Yes, but not clearly. He couldn't see well enough to say who was there. When he found Desi, she was already dead."

"And you believe him?"

"Yes, I do."

"Then I guess the sheriff and I have some questioning to do."

He turned and stalked back down the hallway.

"He's not himself today," I murmured, and Cade's hands moved from my shoulders to my face, cupping my jaw gently, forcing me to look at him.

"I don't care about Dennis. I want to know how you really felt when Devlin kissed you."

His jealousy was obvious and endearing, and I

wondered if he'd heard anything else Dennis and I had said after learning that Devlin kissed me.

"Well?" he prodded.

"It didn't feel like anything, really. It felt like lips on mine, and he said he suspected I wasn't Desi as soon as he kissed me. So I suppose my mouth made no more impression on him than his did on me."

"What a fool," he murmured, as he lowered his lips to mine, catching me in a kiss that pushed every other thought from my head.

****

Richard was in the foyer when I returned to Almenara that evening, and he greeted me cordially, if somewhat stiffly. I regretted the loss of our easy conversation and the warmth that had danced in his eyes prior to my leaving Almenara, and I wondered at the coldness I now sensed in him. I hoped we could still be friends, even if nothing else.

"Richard, won't you please stay for tea?" I asked. "I'd like to discuss Devlin's progress with you."

"I've already discussed it with Eleanor and Lorraine. I'm sure they will update you when they update the sheriff."

He picked up his bag, and turned toward the door, but stopped just short of opening it. With a sigh, he faced me once more.

"I will join you for a cup of tea if you promise we'll discuss only topics of which murder and madness are not a part."

I nodded my agreement, and led him into Desdemona's morning room. I did not feel up to the task of dealing with either Lorraine or Eleanor, and I felt certain no one should disturb us there.

We carried on a casual conversation regarding the sudden coolness in the air and the coming winter, as well as the deliciousness of the cookies Mrs. Hartley had provided. Although casual, the silence that lurked between our words was not as companionable as I had hoped it would be.

Finally, he stood and walked to the mantel, where he studied the picture in earnest.

"I frequently walk the shore in the early morning. I saw Desdemona there so many days, her feet dangling through the openings in the railing, as if she had no fear at all of falling."

"Desi never had much fear of anything." I gave a self-deprecating smile. "I was just the opposite. While Desi ran headlong into whatever she wanted, I was frightened of everything."

"I think your sister was afraid just before her death."

"Why?" I could hardly fathom the idea. Had she somehow known what was coming?

"I was here a few nights before she died. Tabitha was ill with a cold and fever, and I had come to check on her. When I came from the nursery, the door to the roof was open. I could hear Desdemona speaking frantically to someone, but I couldn't make out what she was saying. I called out to her, wanting to speak to her about Tabitha, and she came back inside right away. She seemed quite agitated, and I never saw who it was she was talking to."

"You have no idea?"

He shook his head. "No. I'm sorry. I regret that I didn't know your sister better, Ophelia. It is my duty as a physician to a child such as Tabitha to provide the parents with some support. I should have acted as a confidant to Desdemona, should have listened to her with an open ear rather than lecturing her on taking Tabitha outside and judging her on things I knew little about."

"I'm sure it wasn't as bad as that," I offered. "From the time we were infants, Desi was quite adept at turning a deaf ear to anything she didn't want to hear."

He turned back to me with a smile. "Perhaps you're right. I've been rather haunted by the thought that I might somehow have saved her, had she only felt confident enough in my friendship to confide in me."

"There is no sense beating yourself up over such a conjecture, Richard. Desdemona was a grown woman, used to getting her way, and had she but asked for help, it would have been freely given her by someone, I'm sure."

"Thank you, Ophelia," he said, taking my hands in his and pulling me into his embrace.

I extricated myself, gently but firmly, and stepped away.

He smiled sadly and shook his head. "Forgive me, Ophelia. It seems I might have fallen in love with you."

"I'm flattered, Richard, but I—"

"There's no need to explain. I only wish it was fear that made you so reluctant. Fear I could overcome. Love I can not." He kissed me gently on the cheek and was gone before I could answer him.

As I turned the doorknob to my room, I suddenly remembered the stack of books beside Desi's bed. Could one of them hold the key to her murder? I pushed open the door to her room slowly, peeking in as if I expected her ghost to be waiting for me there.

A chill rushed up my spine as I snatched up the books and practically ran to my room. I was becoming as silly and superstitious as Kathleen had been, I thought.

Most of the books were the same sort of penny novels that Desdemona and I had loved when we were young. My father had called them melodramatic drivel, but Desi and I had read them anyway, finding great pleasure in them through the years.

At the bottom of the stack, I found two somewhat surprising tomes. The first was a tattered and worn Bible that I recognized at once as the one my father had kept on the shelf in his room. It had been the only one of my mother's books he hadn't passed along to us.

I opened it now, running my fingers along the familiar passages. My father must have given it to her when she left home, and I sincerely hoped she had found comfort there in her last days.

The second was a small book of Shakespearean quotes. Inside the front cover, someone had written, "But I will wear my heart upon my sleeve for daws to peck at: I am not what I am." It wasn't Desdemona's handwriting, and only a single initial followed the quote. Whether the single letter signified her or Devlin I had no idea, but the quote from Othello fit them both well enough.

It was no proof of murder or motive, however, and with a weary sigh I put it down and moved to my bureau.

"Well, little dove," I said as I changed into my nightgown, "Every day I have more questions and no answers at all."

Desi had always let her birds walk about the floor,

flying from one low object to the other. She claimed this strengthened them and prepared them to brave the outdoors again. I imagined the mourning dove would enjoy being free of her box, and I crossed the room to lift her out.

My hands flew to my mouth, and I stifled a screech of horror. The poor little thing lay on her back, the pin of a silver brooch driven straight through her tiny heart. Her eyes were sightless and her body already cold when I lifted her out. It took me only a moment to realize that the pin in her chest was not mine. The swallow's topaz eye glinted at me wickedly as I removed Desi's brooch from the tiny body.

Fear jolted through me when I realized someone had come into my room, killed my poor little dove, and left her there for me to find. It was far too similar to the bird I'd found on Desi's dressing table for me to think it wasn't connected.

Whoever it was had known that Desi's brooch would mean something to me. Had someone overheard me telling Cade that our father called me his mourning dove and Desi his barn swallow? Had they placed the dead swallow on Desdemona's bureau and left the dove for me to find because of that? Or had they known it all along? Had the person who killed Desdemona been someone she'd confided in about her life before she came to Almenara? Someone who might not have been her lover, but close enough to be her confidant?

The answer came to me in an instant, and I sank to my bed. My body trembled with the horrible realization that I knew who had killed my sister and it was someone I had never suspected.

Before I could think what to do, Lorraine burst into

my room, her face pale as death and her hands shaking wildly. Tears streamed down her face.

"Eleanor is gone!" she cried. "Devlin has taken her away."

"Where's Calvin?" I was on my feet in an instant, forcing my fear and horror away as I faced the crisis at hand.

"He's gone out looking for her."

"If you see him before I do, tell him to get to the lighthouse," I ordered, throwing my cloak on over my nightgown.

"Where are you going?"

Lorraine was nearing hysteria, and, more than anything, I needed her calm enough to get her husband to the lighthouse as quickly as possible. I grasped her by the shoulders.

"Lorraine, listen to me! You have to tell him to come to the lighthouse. He should bring men with him. Do you understand me?"

She nodded, and I hoped she would remember my command as I rushed down the stairs with her on my heels.

We had barely made it into the foyer when Mrs. Hartley came through the front door.

"They've found her," Mrs. Hartley said. Her face was ashen and her lips trembled as she spoke. "She's on the rocks, as we feared she would be."

Lorraine screamed in anguish, and I grasped her waist to keep her from falling to the floor.

"There's been a mistake," I said as Lorraine buried her head in my shoulder. "It can't be Eleanor."

"There's no mistake, Miss Garrett. Dennis Ames brought the news. He says the men are with her now."

"Mrs. Hartley, please see to Lorraine. I am going to try to catch Dennis before he leaves."

"Yes, miss," she said, taking the sobbing woman into her arms.

I rushed outside, intent on reaching the lighthouse, but the sight of Dory standing still as death in the courtyard brought me to a stop. She stared vacantly out toward the beach, her face unnaturally pale, and tears pouring from her eyes.

I ran to her, wrapped my hands around her arms and tried to reassure her.

"Dory, we must be strong. Perhaps there has been some mistake. I am going there now, to make certain it's Eleanor and not some other poor soul. Dory?"

I shook her once more, and, for the first time, she seemed to register my presence.

"Miss Garrett," she murmured, holding out her hand. In it, she held a single sheet of paper that matched that I'd seen in Desdemona's desk. Foreboding swept through me, and I unfolded it quickly. I gasped as I read the quote from Hamlet, a confession of guilt written in the same script as the handkerchief but far more ominous.

'Tis now the very witching time of night,
when churchyards yawn and hell itself breathes out
Contagion to this world: now could I drink hot
blood.
And so such bitter business as the day
Would quake to look on.

"Where is he, Dory?" I urged.

"He's gone back to the lighthouse, miss." She began to sob hysterically. "I'm so sorry. He told me he loved me, that he would marry me after the trial. I only had to help him scare you away. He told me that Mr. Cade was guilty of murder, and he was afraid you'd find a way to help him get away with it. He said maybe you'd helped him kill her. That you and Mr. Cade were lovers before he married Mrs. Desi. I didn't believe him, at first, but then Susan said she caught you kissing him. And when I saw you two together, I knew you had feelings for each other. I still wouldn't have hurt you, but he told me all I had to do was cry in the night and make you think the house was haunted. I didn't see any harm in it. After Devlin took you to the lighthouse, I told him maybe Mr. Cade wasn't guilty and we should stop trying to prove he was. That's when he got furious at me and told me he never wanted to see me again. I tried to make it up to him when you came back. I led you to the roof so you would find the little bird, but I knew nothing we did was going to make you leave again."

Betrayal ripped through me. I had considered Dory my friend in some ways, and to think she had conspired against me was more than a little hurtful.

"I never thought he'd hurt Miss Eleanor, or poor little Kathleen."

She dabbed her eyes with a handkerchief from her pocket, and I saw the familiar blue monogram on the edge.

"Oh, Dory, what have you done?" I asked, my voice a horrified whisper. "You've helped kill them all."

"No!" she cried in denial, but I didn't wait to listen as I rushed toward the lighthouse.

Chapter Twenty-Eight

Driven by panic, I dashed down the shore to the jetty rocks that surrounded the lighthouse. If Devlin was not already dead, it was only a matter of time. As soon as word of another murder made it to town, the men would converge on the lighthouse to mete out the judgment I had stolen from them only days before.

I expected to see Calvin and the men from Almenara gathered about the rocks where Eleanor lay, but the beach surrounding the lighthouse was empty save for Eleanor, whose body lay crumpled and broken upon the lighthouse rocks. I could see nothing but her legs, which lay at awkward angles, but I knew there was no help for her, and I turned away.

"Dennis!" I shouted, my voice echoing across land and sea, as I spun around. "Dennis!"

He came from behind me, locking his arm around my waist before I knew he was there. I gasped when I felt the gun barrel digging into my side.

"Don't make another sound," he murmured.

"What have you done, Dennis?" I cried. "Why?"

"I told you to be quiet." He emphasized his words with swift jabs of the gun, and I fought a dizzying wave of fear.

Devlin appeared on the beach, staggering toward us from the direction of the cemetery.

"Ophelia!" Devlin gasped. "Run!"

"It's too late for that," Dennis sneered as he lifted the gun and fired.

The bullet pierced Devlin's heart, and as he fell, his glazed eyes met mine. I don't know if he saw me or my sister in those final seconds of life, I only know that her name was the last on his lips, just as it had been for my mother so many years before.

"Have you killed him then, Denny boy?" A man yelled from the top of the dunes, and Dennis puffed out his chest with pride as a group of men came into view behind him.

"Too late for poor Eleanor, I'm afraid," he told them.

"But she'll be the last, won't she?" another man observed as he walked past Devlin's body.

Dennis didn't answer as he backed toward the door of the lighthouse, his arm a vise around my waist.

Down the beach, a small group of men were coming toward us from the direction of Almenara. I recognized Calvin in the front, but my mind could hardly comprehend the sight of Cade running beside him.

"Ophelia!" Cade yelled, picking up speed, when he saw me.

"Cade!" I lunged forward but stilled when Dennis whispered in my ear.

"I'll kill him just like I did Devlin."

I don't know if it was my stillness that gave it away or if, when I moved, Cade saw the gun at my waist, but something alerted him to the danger I was in. I knew it by the way he stumbled slightly, then with a yell, continued to rush toward us. The click of the hammer stopped him in his tracks a few feet away from us. One twitch of Dennis' finger could end my life, and I felt my knees buckle with fear.

"If you faint, I'll kill you both," Dennis murmured.

The calm, cold threat terrified me, and I forced myself to get hold of my emotions.

Calvin had reached his sister's body, and I saw him crouch down beside her, his shoulders bowed with grief. Even considering the fight I'd witnessed between them a few days ago, I did not doubt his grief. If there was anyone who understood the love-hate relationship that often existed between siblings, it was I.

"Dennis, get over here!" Calvin snapped without looking up, but Dennis just chuckled.

"I don't think so, Sheriff."

Calvin looked toward us, ready to lay into his subordinate, but Cade stilled him with an uplifted hand.

"Stay calm, Cal. He's got a gun to her side. He'll kill her."

"Very observant, Cade," Dennis mocked. "Too bad you weren't quite so in tune with your wife. Perhaps you could have saved her. At the very least, you could have saved the others."

"Even if you kill her, you'll never get away with it," Cade promised him.

"Of course I won't. You and Calvin will hunt me down, run me to ground, and shoot me. But it won't bring Ophelia back."

I knew it was hopeless, then. He had already decided he was going to kill me, despite the consequences.

"You've lost her again, Cade," he said, before pulling me into the darkened interior of the lighthouse and barring the door from the inside.

As Dennis dragged me up the stairs, I could hear Cade yelling my name while he and the others attempted to break through the door.

Dennis pushed me onto the parapet, where I stumbled across the uneven stone and caught myself on the railing. The sky was the deep purplish gray of the pre-dawn hours, and the sound of the gulls flying over the bay wafted toward us. I wondered how often Desi had seen the world look like this. How often had she found solace from her loveless marriage here, as the rest of the world slept? I was sorry she had found the love she had sought all her life only at the end of it. I wanted her to know I loved her, and I had always imagined her as happily married. Despite my love for Cade, or maybe because of it, I would never have wished them the misery they had endured.

I closed my eyes as a soft wind brushed my face with coolness, and I made peace with my sister at last. I imagined I could hear her laughter on the wind and feel her arms wrapping me in a gentle embrace.

It was a beautiful morning, and if it was to be the morning I met my Maker, then I would do so with a heart free of bitterness and hurt.

"Your sister fought like a wildcat," Dennis mocked as he grabbed me by the arm. "She was right. You are the meeker one."

"Perhaps my sister wasn't sure what her future held. I am."

"She knew her future held death. You're certainly smart enough to realize yours holds the same thing."

I have no idea how I found what felt like a peaceful smile and, in spite of my terror, spoke in an amazingly calm voice. "Death is only a step into a new sort of future, Dennis."

He grunted out his opinion of my lack of fear, as well as my faith, as he wrapped his fingers in my hair and forced my head down, over the railing, so I could see the rocks below. The world seemed to tilt crazily toward me, the sky and the ground spinning in tandem, but I refused to show him my fear. Instead, I dug my fingers into the cold hard stone, steadying my mind and my body with a force of will I hadn't known I had.

"You loved her, didn't you?" I asked, turning my face toward the man at my side.

He pulled me upright, his face mottled with emotion.

"Did she love you?"

His reserve broke then, and he seemed to deflate into the boy I had known during my first few days at Almenara.

"Yes, I loved her, and she loved me. Until Devlin came along, that is. Then she cast me aside like a broken toy."

"That's how she was, Dennis. She did it to me, to Cade, to you. It was her way."

"She never loved Cade," he bit out.

"But she pretended to. She made him love her."

"No, she said even though he married her, he never loved her. He still loved you. That's why she turned to me. She was so sad and alone, so hurt by the fact that he couldn't love her."

I shook my head. "She always knew what to say to get her way, Dennis. She always knew how to talk to men. Before Cade, it was my father she said didn't love her."

He jabbed my chest with the gun that was still in

his hand.

"Don't talk about her like that. Susan talked about her, you know. Said she was no different than any two-bit whore. Said it obviously ran in the family, because she'd seen you and Cade kissing beside Desdemona's coffin." He looked proud of himself when he added, "But I took care of her. She won't be spreading any more of her filthy lies."

"You killed Desi," I told him. "You couldn't have cared about her."

"You don't know what you're talking about. I cared more than anyone."

"Ophelia!" Cade roared from below us. "Show me your face!"

I tried to lean forward to let him see I was fine, but Dennis tightened his grip in my hair. "You let him sit down there and rot with worry. This isn't about him!"

"Of course not. It's about you, Dennis. How much you cared for my sister. How badly she hurt you."

"Yes, that's right. I did care for her. I didn't mean to kill her." He spoke quickly, erratically, panting as if his heart might beat from his chest at any moment. "I followed her up here one morning. I just wanted to talk, to make her tell me why she quit loving me, but she was so angry I was here, she yelled and screamed at me, told me she loved Devlin, and I was nothing but a child. She told me I had to leave. She said she never loved me at all."

He took a deep shuddering breath and closed his eyes as if trying to block out the memory of that moment.

"I hit her, backhanded her so hard she lost her balance and fell against the railing. She screamed out

Devlin's name. Even then, when all her attention should have been on me, she yelled out his name, not mine. My handprint was on her face, and there was a trickle of blood from her lip where I'd hit her. She looked so young and scared. I went to her, trying to tell her how sorry I was, but she screamed again, and tried to run away from me. I caught her by the hair and dragged her back to me. She went crazy, then. She fought with all her might, but she wasn't that strong. I was able to get hold of both her hands and pin her to the wall. She kept a few of Cade's ties here to secure Tabby to her when they sat on the edge. She used the collars to wipe her face and hands. I swear I was only trying to stop her from fighting when I bound her hands with one of the cravats. I don't know why I covered her eyes. I was only trying to make her calm down. It worked, too. She calmed down right away. So I pulled her against me, tried to hold her in my arms and tell her I loved her. But she said she hated me and swore she would burn in hell before she'd ever let me touch her again. I don't remember throwing her over. One minute she was in my arms and the next she was gone. She didn't even scream as she fell."

He let go of my hair and looked over the railing. I stepped toward him, thinking if I could catch him off guard I could push him over. He was faster than I was, however, and had me back against him, the gun pointed at my head, in a heartbeat.

"I'm surprised at you, Ophelia. I didn't know I could fill your kind, compassionate heart with enough hatred to want to kill. Self-preservation is a powerful thing, I suppose."

Below us, I heard the door finally give way and

booted feet pounded up the stairs. Cade burst through the door, stopping short when he saw the gun at my head.

"You've told me about Desi and Susan, but what about Kathleen and Eleanor? What could they possibly have done to make you kill them?"

"Kathleen was so certain she'd heard Desi crying in the night, so certain her ghost walked the corridors of Almenara. She came to the lighthouse looking for the answers it would take to put Desi's spirit to rest. I was here courting demons of my own when she came through the door. She was dressed in a white gown, and with all that black hair flying about her face, I thought she was Desdemona come back to haunt me. I admit I was terrified, and when she started toward me, I panicked. She was on the rocks before I even knew what happened. It was her screaming that made me realize it wasn't Desi, and by that time it was too late. Her screams alerted Devlin, and he came running onto the beach as she hit the rocks below. He wasn't picking her pockets when the men found him, he was checking to see if she was alive."

He exhaled wearily and relaxed his grip on my waist a bit. I wondered what would happen once he tired of talking. Would he shoot me or throw me over the edge? There was no way I would survive either alternative, so I tried to keep him talking.

"Eleanor?" I coaxed.

"Ah, Eleanor, sweet, romantic little Eleanor. She was so convinced Devlin loved her and if she could just get him safely away from here, they would live happily ever after. I caught them headed out of town. He was nearly unconscious, and she was so desperate to save

244

him, she was practically carrying him on her back. I offered them a ride, and once I had them in the wagon, I brought them to the cemetery. He was too weak to do a thing about it when I left him lying there and dragged her away. I had every intention of killing her, just for the fun of it, actually, but nature beat me to it. She'd already worn herself out carrying him down the road, and I suppose this climb, as well as fear, took their toll on her. When we reached the top, her face turned a ghastly purple color and she collapsed in a heap. She wasn't the most slender of girls, and it was a bit of an effort to toss her body over, but I managed it."

He pressed his face against my cheek, his breath hot on my skin, just below the spot where the cold steel of the gun pressed against my temple.

"And you're no different from the rest, wanting Cade despite thinking he killed your sister, kissing Devlin to get what you wanted, a little spy and a sniping gossip. You deserve to die just as they did."

"Did you kill my dove?" Not that the dove was so important in the grand scheme of things, but I needed to keep him talking.

"Of course I killed it. I gave it to you and then I killed it. Desi had given Devlin Lorraine's cloak to keep him warm, but she forgot to remove her brooch. I stole it from him while I played nursemaid this morning. That poor little bird hardly made a sound when I stabbed it through its heart. I knew you'd get the message."

"Fee," Cade said quietly from the doorway, and I locked my eyes on his.

Relief swept through me as I realized I had done what I set out to do. I had proven that Cade wasn't a murderer. He hadn't killed Desi or anyone else. He was free to live his life without suspicion.

"Ophelia," he said sternly, his dark eyes never leaving mine, "it's not over yet."

"Oh, but it is," Dennis said, pushing himself up and over the side of the parapet in one sudden movement. I screamed as my feet left the ground, and I was certain I was going over.

"No!" Cade lunged toward us, just as Dennis loosened his grip on me and hurtled toward the rocky ground below. Cade's arm caught me by the waist and carried me to the stone floor beside him.

Breathing raggedly, we got to our feet, clinging to each other tightly as the men who had come up with him went back down to see to Dennis's body.

"I thought I'd lost you again," he murmured against my hair.

"Never again," I whispered, lifting my face for his kiss. "I'm here to stay."

Around us, a gentle wind picked up as the sun began to rise over the horizon, and Desdemona's laughter blended with the call of the birds in flight. The past and present met in the familiar depths of Cade's dark eyes, my regret fell away, and I faced my future without bitterness or regret.

Chapter Twenty-Nine

"Oh, Ophelia, you are a sight to behold," Mrs. Dupree exclaimed as she straightened the white, handmade lace so that it lay perfectly over the silk underskirt. "Your father would be so proud of you."

Dory pinned the last few wayward curls to the top of my head before securing my veil and stepping back to survey me.

"You've never looked more beautiful, Miss Fee," she said, and I gave her a quick hug. Although Cade had wanted to dismiss her after learning her part in Dennis' deception, I had convinced him Dory was a victim as well, and he had agreed to keep her on.

John Bailey waited on the church steps, and his wise old eyes welled up with tears when he saw me. I placed my hand on his arm as the doors swung open before us.

I scanned the sea of familiar, smiling faces. I had insisted Cade and I wait the appropriate amount of time before announcing our engagement, but he had agreed to wait only half of it. I needn't have feared how his short mourning period would be perceived. It seemed everyone who knew us was ready to have us married by year's end.

The servants were grouped together in the back few rows of the church, and I offered each of them a smile and nod as we passed. Mrs. Hartley's stoic face was wreathed with a smile, while tears ran freely down her cheeks.

Nellie stood near the front of the church, her tiny blond daughter in her arms. At six months old, the child was a miniature version of Nellie but with Reverend Arnold's solemn brown eyes and nearly bald head, and she studied me so intently I had to stifle a laugh.

Lorraine and Calvin were in the row in front of Nellie, their hands wound tightly together and half-smiles on their faces. Deeply distraught over Eleanor's death, Calvin had given up his badge the day after her funeral and purchased a home far from the place his former wife and sister died. Although we had little contact with them, the tension between Calvin and Cade seemed to have lessened and they could be in the same room without any threat of altercation.

Feeling his eyes on me, I looked toward Cade, who stood beneath a flowered arch at the front of the church. Sunlight streamed through the stained glass window behind him, burnishing him with red and gold, like an ancient god come to collect his bride. My breath caught in my throat at the love burning in his dark eyes and the wild beat of the pulse at his throat.

I felt the blush that stole over my skin as I imagined pressing my lips there, feeling the steady rhythm of it against my mouth. In just a few short hours, I would be with him as I had never been with anyone before. Cade's low chuckle told me he knew what I was thinking as John placed my hand in his and we turned to Reverend Arnold. Within minutes, I was no longer Ophelia Garrett, the spinster daughter of Reverend Garrett, and I faced the congregation a married woman.

Clinging to Cade's hand, I followed him down the aisle, past the smiling faces of those who loved us, and into the bright afternoon sun.

The trees between the church and cemetery were in full bloom, and a bright blue swallow sat on the railing of the iron fence behind them. Twittering happily, it flew off to join a small flock already in flight, and I could well imagine the ghosts of Almenara being carried away on their wings and the soft spring wind.

A word about the author...

Gloria Davidson Marlow is the author of several romantic suspense novels. She resides in Northeast Florida with her husband, works as a paralegal at a local law firm, and spends as much time as possible with her three grandsons.

Previous Releases

SWEET SACRIFICES
available from The Wild Rose Press, Inc.

~

Flowers for Megan
Shades of Silence
The Butterfly Game
available elsewhere